The Einstein Solution

The Einstein Solution
Published by Mischievous Muse Press
A subsidiary of The World Nouveau Company
Los Angeles County, California

Cover design by Gineve Lynnara

Library of Congress Cataloging-in-Publication Data
Shriver, Jean Adair
The Einstein Solution/Jean Adair Shriver

Intermediate Fiction

Mischievous Muse Press/ World Nouveau Company

ISBN: 987-0-9828865-2-6

10 9 8 7 6 5 4 3

Printed in the United States of America

With thanks to the Millie Ames Writing Workshop for their help and support. Also thanks to Cat and Gineve who had a good idea when they thought up Mischievous Muse!

The Einstein Solution

Jean Adair Shriver

Author's Note

The Einstein Solution is fictional, but there are true things in it. I really did grow up in Princeton, New Jersey. And I really did live right across the street from Albert Einstein. Most mornings as I was walking to school, he'd pass me as he walked to work but I never spoke to him, because he was a famous mathematician and I was a girl who could barely do long division.

Other parts of this story are also based on truth. Before World War II, Princeton was a small town where most people knew each other. When the war started our fathers and brothers left to join the Army or Navy or Marines. New people moved into town. People who seemed different than the people we'd always known. Princeton wasn't used to strangers.

Like Miss Worth's School, my school was for girls only. When a girl showed up who looked different or dressed different, I'm afraid we weren't very welcoming. I never knew anyone called Kat Goodman, but I remember how my friends and I either ignored new arrivals or were sometimes rude to them. Once, a frustrated newcomer called Ann yelled at us, "Jesus Christ wouldn't treat people like you do!" Though I tried to laugh off her remark, I was deeply ashamed of myself. Ann, this book is for you.

--JS

Monday, April 6, 1942
Japanese Land Close to India
R.A.F. Loses 15 Planes in Big Raids

Chapter One

I heard Miss Sowerby's oxfords clump down the stairs. The headmistress strode over to where my class was lined up for Phys. Ed. "I need a volunteer," she said.

Twenty hands shot up. Anything—pulling weeds, delivering messages, dusting books—was better than climbing ropes in a gym that smelled like B.O.

"A new student has arrived from California. I want one of you to welcome her to Miss Worth's."

The minute she said "California" Lucy and Mona dropped their hands. So did the rest of their club. Only my hand was still waving in the air.

Sowerby spotted it. "Ah, thank you, Rosemary. You'll find Enid Goodman in the front hall."

As she bustled away, someone hissed. Must be Mona. She hissed a lot.

"Lucy," I turned to the girl who used to be my best friend, "what's going on?"

"You'll find out." Lucy flipped her blonde pageboy over her shoulder and turned her back on me. These days she wouldn't even answer my questions.

In the front hall I slipped behind a column to spy on Enid Goodman. The new girl sat on a bench under the portrait of Miss Worth draped in a big fur and three strands of pearls. She was wearing a cream wool suit. On the jacket was pinned a beautiful circle of gold roses.

The new girl had dark fuzzy eyebrows. Her mouth was set in a straight line. She looked nothing like the smiling California girls in magazines. Her hair was dark brown and curly. Amazing. Except for me every girl in Class Eight had a smooth pageboy which they rolled in socks each night.

I ran one hand over my own curls, took a deep breath and stepped out. "Hi, I'm Rosemary Hoyt. What a great tan. Are you really from California?"

"I'm from Beverly Hills." She talked through her nose which made her voice sound like a duck quacking. "My father's producing films for the government. There's a war on you know."

My face got hot. "Of course I know. My father's in the Navy. He . . ." Omigod, the girl was yawning. Right in my face. How rude can you get? I pasted on a fake smile. "Welcome to Miss Worth's, Enid."

The girl scowled. "I hate that name. Call me Kat with a K."

"Sure, er . . . Kat. Well, I'm supposed to show you around. The classrooms are all on the second floor, so let's go." I pointed to the wide white stairs.

Kat put one hand on the bench and pushed herself to her feet. One of her knees didn't bend right. Her eyes stared at me, hard as green marbles. She was daring me to ask about her leg.

Somehow I managed to keep my mouth shut and led the way upstairs.

At the top, I turned, "Our homeroom teacher's Mrs. Hazeltine. She's our English teacher too. She's really nice." Kat raised her dark eyebrows. I babbled on. "Her husband's on an aircraft carrier in the Pacific."

Kat made a sour face. "I hate English." She walked stiffly down the hall.

2

I caught up. "It's my favorite subject." Craning my neck to look at her face. "How old are you?"

"Fifteen." My mouth dropped open. She turned red and mumbled, ". . . had to repeat eighth grade."

"Because of . . .?" I glanced at her leg.

Kat pressed her lips together and shrugged.

Sowerby stuck her head out of her office. "Introduce Enid to Mrs. Hazeltine, Rosemary."

Kat limped along beside me, "I hate reading. Dad used to bring me movies from the studio when I had to do book reports. The last one he brought home was *National Velvet.* The movie was okay, even if Elizabeth Taylor is a brat."

"You know Elizabeth Taylor?" I knew my eyes were popping.

"She comes to my birthday parties." Kat leaned against the wall breathing in puffs like walking was hard work for her. "At least I get to take science . . . while you're stuck in gym."

"Science? Oh poor you. Miss Stockbridge is sooo strict. And she looks kind of scary with those yellow teeth and her weird yellow curls that look like snails."

"Who cares what she looks like?" Kat said.

I blushed, then called to a girl coming down the hall. "Hey Adelaide, this is . . ."

Adelaide brushed past us and hurried away. Why wouldn't she say hello to Kat? Was it her clothes?

At Miss Worth's we didn't have uniforms, but all the girls wore the same kind of Shetland sweaters buttoned up the back, Peter Pan collars, plaid skirts, knee socks and loafers. Kat's clothes were lovely, but different. Should I tip her off or would she figure it out for herself?

The day dragged on. It was tough being stuck with somebody everyone ignored. When our last class finished, I took Kat out to the front porch where girls waited for their rides.

"Before the war, I could walk to school," I explained, "but when Daddy joined the Navy, we had to move in with my grandfather and he lives way out in the country and . . ."

"Louis, I'm up here!" Kat broke in, waving to a car below. She limped down the steps. A man in a dark uniform opened the door of a black limousine. Kat flicked her hand at me and was gone.

"Typical rude behavior," Lucy said in my ear. "My dad says they trample over everyone."

"Huh?"

"And my mother," Lucy smoothed her black velvet hair band, "says now that Miss Sowerby has let one in, we'll have a flood."

"A flood of what?"

"Jews, stupid. Honestly, Rosemary, can't you put two and two together? Goodman. Movie people. Where are your brains?"

Lucy couldn't put two and two together without a math tutor, but because she was finally talking to me, I didn't say that.

"Hey, I don't know any Jews," I tried to smile, "except Albert Einstein who used to live across the street from me."

"Einstein doesn't count. Besides, he doesn't go to our school."

I couldn't help giggling. "Can't you see him walking down the halls, smoking his stinky old pipe?"

Lucy gave one tee hee, then stopped and said crossly, "Oh grow up, Rosemary." Throwing open her blazer, she raised her face to the sun, "God, le *pringtemp est mairvelooze*."

Lucy's mangled French got me giggling again. She whipped around and stuck her face in mine. "What's she like?"

"Who? Kat?"

"I thought her name was Enid."

"She wants to be called Kat."

"Quite buddy-buddy, you two." Lucy opened a small compact and peered at the mirror. "My mother says they rented a huge house." She dabbed on pink lipstick. "My dad says all Jews throw their money around. Don't you think having a chauffeur is *tres noovo rich*?"

"I guess," I said, feeling uncomfortable. I twisted my curly hair into a thick rope. "Lucy, my grandfather's cat just had kittens. Want to come see them?"

Lucy's sharp face relaxed. "I'd love to," she said in her old voice. Then, as Mona slithered up, hissing softly, Lucy gave a fake laugh. "Silly girl, I'm insanely busy. Besides," she frowned, "my mother wouldn't let me come. She's mad at your grandfather. For being against the war."

Tears clouded my eyes and I was really glad to see our old Ford convertible turn into the driveway. Gathering up my books, I said, "Honestly Lucy, I'm not buddy-buddy with Kat."

"No?" Lucy's right eyebrow rose. "You still want to join our club?"

"Oh yes, yes I do, oh yes please." In Miss Worth's eighth grade, if you weren't in Lucy and Mona's club, you might as well be dead.

Lucy's eyes twinkled. "*Ma chair*, I've got a great initiation stunt for you."

"Huh?"

"Don't gape, Rosemary. *Fermay la bush.*"

"It's pronounced boosh."

A frown line appeared between Lucy's eyebrows. "Dammit, Rosemary, do you want to join or not?"

"I do, but I have to go now." Standing up. "My mother's here."

Lucy grabbed my shoulder. "Here's your assignment."

Whatever it was—swim the Delaware, snitch a Hershey bar from Woolworth's, talk back to Miss Sowerby—I'd do it.

"Make friends with Enid Goodman," said Lucy.

I gasped. "I can't! She doesn't like me."

Lucy's smile showed the chipped tooth she got playing Kick the Can in fourth grade. "Come on, Rosemary, I want you in the club. I've missed you."

Those words felt like warm butterscotch sliding over my sore heart. "Okay, but if you don't like Jews, then why . . . ?"

Mum honked and yelled out the window, "Rosemary, please!"

"Just do it," Lucy said, "and we'll vote you in."

Monday, April 6, 1942
Langley Aircraft Carrier Sunk by Japanese
U.S. Flying Fortresses Bomb Fleet Off Burma

Chapter Two

I slid into the front seat of our old car. Daddy named it Theophilus, "because it's the awfullest car in town." My younger brother Jackie sat in back drawing with a pencil on a big pad. Mum's cigarette smoke was making him cough.

Mum looked at me. "Was that Lucy Lavalle sitting with you on the porch?"

"Yes."

She smiled. "Good. I was afraid you were losing touch with your old friends."

I didn't want her to know I was an outcast with my old friends. "Well, it takes a lot of gas to get out to Teddy's house. And gas is rationed."

"I know." Mum's shoulders slumped. "I didn't want to move in with Father, but we couldn't afford the rent on our house now that Daddy's gone." She looked really sad.

Flashing my best Shirley Temple smile, I said, "Lucy promised me that soon I'd be getting into her club."

"Oh I'm delighted." Mum lit another Chesterfield, though she already had one burning in the ashtray. Cigarettes were really scarce, but Mum was smoking more than ever. "Your father will be so glad. We both know how important it is to stay on the good side of the people who count in Princeton."

I stubbed out her first cigarette before she set the ashtray on fire. Mum was always saying things like that. I hadn't told her about being left out of Lucy's club, because I knew she'd worry. But today was a breakthrough. All I had to do was make friends with Kat Goodman and I'd be in.

"Do you know any Jews?" I said.

"Goodness Rosemary, I'm much too busy for silly questions like that. I'm the only one around to make sure you and Jackie do your homework, get enough sleep and eat your food."

"I'd eat more food if you did the cooking," said Jackie in a whiny voice.

I nodded. Teddy was the only person in town who didn't complain about wartime meat rationing. My grandfather was a vegetarian and every night he made a different casserole. On good nights he put cheese in them. On bad nights he added slimy things I didn't dare ask about.

"To answer your question," Mum turned to me, "I don't know any Jews."

Now we were driving down the street where we used to live. Passing our brick house gave me a lump in my throat. But today I saw something that made me grin.

"Mum," I yelled, "you do so know a Jew! You know Albert Einstein. And there he is walking home from work, like he does every day." Baggy blue sweater, wispy white hair hanging over his collar, sandals with no socks. Everything else in my life had changed, but Einstein had stayed the same.

Mum frowned. "I don't know Professor Einstein. I've never even talked to him."

"Me neither. What would I say to a famous mathematician? I can barely do long division."

Mum rubbed a thin hand over her forehead. "Be quiet, Rosemary. Let me think."

"About what?"

"Gas rationing. If we don't get more coupons, we won't be able to get you children to school."

"Yippee!" Jackie threw his pad in the air.

I glanced at what he'd been drawing and my eyes went wide.

"Mum," I yelled, "Jackie's drawing Nazi tanks again. Make him stop."

"I have to draw that stuff. The Nazis are going to win," he shouted, face red and tears in his eyes.

I grabbed his drawing and tore it up. "They're not going to win the war, you idiot!"

Jackie started blubbering. "We've got these maps at school. The teachers put pins in them. Our side doesn't have as many pins as Hitler and the Japs."

"Enough," Mum said, "Rosemary," she lowered her voice, "go easy on him." Her smile was crooked. "Your brother's a pessimist like me. You're like your father—optimistic."

That shut me up for the rest of the ride. When Mum stopped the car in front of Teddy's barn, I ran in to check on the baby kittens.

Holding the black and white one against my cheek, I murmured, "We are not going to lose the war. We are going to win. And I am going to get into Lucy's club very soon."

At dinner Mum put one elbow on the table and read a book while she ate. Teddy came out of the kitchen wearing a red checked apron over his suit. He handed us plates of what looked like gray jellyfish and boiled carrots. Jackie stared at the food in horror. I tried not to gag. Mum kept telling us, "Don't complain about the food. It's very good of Father to take us in."

I looked at Teddy's crisp white mustache and bright blue eyes. He was a Princeton professor and very smart. And yet he was doing this dumb thing of going around telling everyone America shouldn't be fighting this war.

"Why?" I had asked him many times.

"I'm a Quaker, Rosemary. Quakers don't believe war settles anything."

Tonight I wasn't going to argue about the war. I leaned across the table and said, "We have a new girl in our class. I think she's Jewish."

Teddy's eyes gleamed. "A refugee? From Germany? Our Friends Service Committee recently smuggled a Jewish family out of Berlin . . ."

"No, she's from California. Her father makes movies."

Teddy looked disappointed.

"Mum," I turned to my mother, "you could invite the Goodmans here, couldn't you?"

"Who?"

"The Jewish girl's family," I explained, "You always say we should be nice to newcomers."

Mum flushed and looked down at her book. "Nobody from Hollywood would . . ."

"Grace," said Teddy sharply, "thee should be truthful with thy children." At home Teddy used the Quaker thee and thou. "Tell thy daughter the real reason thee won't invite them."

Mum's chin went up. "I think people are more comfortable sticking with their own kind." She glared at Teddy. "Besides, it's wartime and nobody is entertaining." Angry red circles popped out on her cheeks.

Teddy shook his head and I ate my carrots. I couldn't handle the jellyfish stuff.

After dinner, I was in my room doing my homework, when I heard Mum and Teddy arguing. They were trying to keep their voices down, but I could hear them.

Teddy. "Thee is willing to fight Hitler, but thee won't welcome Jews to this house."

Mum. "Nobody in Princeton wants Jews moving into our town."

Teddy. "So thee won't invite Rosemary's friend here?"

Mum's voice sounded squeaky. "You don't care what people think, but I do." I could tell she was crying.

I got up to shut my door and found Jackie standing there.

He held out his Chinese checkers board. "Play with me?" His big eyes glistened behind his glasses. One tuft of light brown hair stood up at the back of his head.

I hardened my heart. "Not till you stop drawing Nazis."

His lower lip trembled. "Rosemary, I don't want them to win. I'm just scared they will." Board under his arm, he shuffled back to his room.

I paced my room feeling nervous. How could I make friends with someone as prickly as Kat? Lucy might as well have asked me to spin straw into gold. At least the girl in that old story had

Rumpelstiltskin for a helper. The only dwarf around here was Jackie and he was useless.

I got down my Webster's Collegiate Dictionary and looked up Jew. "Orig. one of the tribe of Judah, hence any person of the Hebrew people or anyone whose religion is Judaism."

I picked up the Bible I got in Sunday school and read about Adam and Eve getting thrown out of Eden and Esau eating his brother's cereal. Not enough information.

Mum's footsteps went down the hall. Teddy came next, clicking out lights.

I waited a few seconds, then opened my door. All was quiet except for the ticking of the downstairs clock. I tiptoed down the steps and into the living room. My hand was on the J volume of the Encyclopedia Britannica, when I heard footsteps.

"It's late, Rosemary." Teddy's bony knees showed below his old-fashioned nightshirt. "Thee should be in bed. Do thy studying in the morning." He put a gentle hand on my shoulder. "As for your Jewish family, any friend of yours is welcome here."

That was nice of Teddy, but it didn't solve my problem. Kat wasn't my friend. Not yet. Would she ever be?

Wednesday, April 8, 1942
75 Japanese Planes Raid Ceylon
40,000 Nazis Shot, Soviet Announces

Chapter Three

On Wednesdays, Miss Worth's School always closed at noon. Everyone walked two blocks uptown for lunch. Through the drizzling spring rain, I saw Kat Goodman limping along the slate sidewalk ahead of me.

"Wait up," I said, "hey Kat, wait up."

Kat Goodman had been at Miss Worth's for two weeks, but so far I'd made no progress getting to know her. Every morning, I'd say hello. She'd grunt. I'd ask if she wanted to eat with me in the cafeteria. She'd shake her head.

Yesterday she told me she ate in the science lab.

I pinched my nose. "Pee-yew, that place stinks of rotten eggs."

Now I caught up to her and pointed to the white dogwoods blooming in front of Holder Hall, one of the University's stone dormitories. "Gorgeous, aren't they?"

Kat looked at me as if I were a talkative bug. "My brother lives there," she pointed to Holder Hall, "he's a Princeton freshman."

I couldn't think of anything to say except "Oh."

Kat went on. "He's the reason we came to live in Princeton instead of New York. Mom wants to keep an eye on him. She's scared he's going to quit college and enlist in the army."

"Gee, you're soooo lucky to have an older brother. My brother is nine and he's an idiot." Kat smiled. Progress, I thought and glanced at her stiff leg. "Rain makes these sidewalks awfully slippery. You . . ." Her rigid face stopped me.

Kat checked her watch. "Gotta meet David in Renwick's."

Clearly she wanted me to vamoose. But like a desperate stray dog, I followed Kat into the coffee shop and sat down beside her.

After a week of Teddy's meatless dinners, the hamburgers smelled divine. Mouth watering, I piled up what I had left of my allowance on the table. A quarter, three dimes and a nickel.

Kat shoved my change back at me. She pulled a five dollar bill out of her wallet. "I'll buy."

My cheeks burned with anger. Maybe Lucy was right about Jews. Maybe they did "throw their money around."

Speaking of Lucy, there she was sitting in a booth with three club girls. I smiled at them and they burst out laughing.

Two boys came over to our table. The one hugging Kat had to be her brother. Wow, did he ever get the looks in their family. Long brown lashes and eyes that sloped down at the outside corners. Brown hair and ivory skin. The other boy was red haired and homely.

"This is David," Kat said grinning at her brother. To David, "Rosemary's in my class."

"Hi, Rosemary."

I opened my mouth, but nothing came out. He was so gorgeous. I couldn't say a word, couldn't even breathe.

"So how's the science fiend?" David asked.

"Fine." Kat blew the paper cover off her straw. It hit his nose.

"Watchit, kiddo!"

Kat laughed, loud as a donkey braying. Everyone turned to look at us. I squirmed. Mum always told me not to make myself "conspicuous" in public. I hoped nobody was going to report this lunch to her.

The waitress, whose sister used to be my baby nurse, came to take our order. Three hamburgers and a tuna sandwich. When she left, David lit a cigarette.

"Smoking's bad for you," Kat said, "raises your blood pressure."

"Hey, kid," David's friend jabbed a finger at Kat, "how do you know that if you don't smoke?"

"Our science teacher lets me take her blood pressure before and after she smokes."

My jaw dropped. *Scary old Miss Stockbridge lets Kat do science experiments on her?*

The redhead clutched a spoon and crooned a song at it. Kat yelled, "Frankie!" and pretended to faint, like she was one of those stupid teenagers with a crush on Frank Sinatra. Heads turned toward our table. I saw my piano teacher purse her lips when she recognized me. Uh oh.

Lucy stood up and pointed to the restroom door at the back. I hurried to meet her.

The toilet in the Ladies Room had this purple light under the seat that was supposed to kill germs. It made everything look spooky. In the mirror, Lucy's skin was chalky and her eyes were dark holes.

She pulled out her lipstick. "Who is he?"

"Who?"

"The gorgeous one, of course."

"You mean the redhead?"

"Rosemary, you're not funny! Come on, tell."

"He's Kat's brother. David Goodman."

Lucy sniffed. "I should have known. My father says they are always loud in public." The purple light made the lipstick on her mouth look black.

I smiled at her. "See how far I've gotten with Kat?"

"Keep working," Lucy said, blotting her mouth with a tissue.

"But . . . when can I . . . ?"

Lucy patted my shoulder, "If it was me, Rosie, you'd be in already. But Mona says . . ."

"Mona!" I jerked away from her. "When did that start? Last year we always called her Pee Wee."

Lucy touched her hair band. "I've called her Mona ever since she got petite and sweet."

13

"When was that?"

"When three Lawrenceville boys invited her to a tea dance."

I wilted. "So how much longer do I have to wait?"

Lucy smiled at the mirror. "That's for us to know and you to find out." She pushed on the door and swished out.

When I got back to the table our food had arrived. Kat and David's hamburgers smelled delicious. My tuna sandwich looked boring.

"How's Mom?" David asked Kat.

"She's driving me crazy with her bawling."

David grinned. "Remember how she cried when you blew up your bathroom at Dad's Oscar party?"

"This is different. Mom's obsessed with finding her Rosenbaum cousins. Dad hired detectives to go to Berlin and search for them. They struck out. Now Hitler's closed the German borders. Nobody can get in and nobody can get out."

"Oh yes they can," I said. Everyone turned to look at me. I blushed.

David fixed his gorgeous eyes on me. "What do you know about Berlin?"

"M-my grandfather's friends just s-smuggled a J-jewish f-family out of there."

David leaned forward. His eyes were the color of horse chestnuts. "No kidding," he said. He turned to Kat. "What's your grandfather's name?"

"Theodore Cope," I said proudly. "He teaches geology at the University."

David's eyes went wide. "Professor Cope? The Quaker? The traitor!"

I nodded, looking down at the table.

The redhead blew a raspberry. "Is he the idiot who says we shouldn't fight Hitler?"

I looked at their angry faces, swallowed and turned away.

David pounded the table. "If you knew what was happening in Germany, you'd see why I call Cope is a traitor. Even Einstein," David said, "quit being a pacifist when he found out what Hitler was doing to Jews. But Cope," he looked as if he'd like to hit me, "aaah I can't talk about it." He threw down some money and stood up.

14

The door banged as David and his friend left. I watched a fly climb over my sandwich crusts.

The silence went on and on.

Finally Kat said, "Why are those girls pointing at us and laughing?"

"What girls?"

"The snobby ones, the pageboy and Peter Pan collar kids."

"Gosh, how would I know?" Trying to look innocent.

"If this is a setup . . ." Kat clenched her jaw and leaned forward. "How come you follow me around so much?"

I cleared my throat. "I-I love meeting new people, and I think California is the neatest place in the country. I want to go there some day. Those girls haven't been anywhere. Don't know anything. They are just hicks."

"This whole town is full of hicks," Kat said, but she unclenched her hands.

"I'm sorry I made your brother mad. See, my . . . my grandfather's a Quaker and they don't believe in war."

Kat sighed. "S'okay. David's like Mom. Too emotional."

"If . . . if you could meet my grandfather, you'd see . . ."

Kat leaned toward me. "I want to."

"What?"

Kat stared up at the cloud of cigarette smoke floating over our heads. "Maybe he could help us. If his Quakers could find Mom's cousins, she'd quit crying. Can you fix it so I can talk to him?"

"Sure," I said grinning, "you bet I can."

Thursday, April 9, 1942
Japanese Capture Bataan,
Sink 2 British Cruisers

Chapter Four

Because Teddy had told me I could invite Kat out to his house, I almost asked her to ride home with me after school. Then I remembered what happened with Mum and Barbara Gates and changed my mind.

It was the summer before fifth grade. All my friends were at camp. I walked to the library every day. That's where I met Barbara. I told her how much I loved *The Secret Garden.* She told me to check out *Little Women.* We'd sit on the library steps and talk.

One scorching morning, I said, "Want to go to The Pretty Brook Club and swim?"

She nodded. Then said she didn't have a bathing suit. I said I'd loan her one.

We walked into my house. "Mum," I called, "can you give us a ride to the club?"

My mother showed up and pulled me into the kitchen. She shut the door in Barbara's face and whispered, "You can't take a little colored girl to the club."

"Why not? She's nice."

"Everyone would stare at her and she'd be uncomfortable."

My throat clogged up. "But I already asked her. What can I say?"

"Tell her the pool is being cleaned. Tell her you don't feel well. Tell her to go home. Now."

Feeling sick, I went back to Barbara. "Um . . . ah . . . see, I forgot . . . ah . . . Friday is the day they clean the pool."

"That's okay," Barbara's smile was cheerful. She put her hands behind her back and looked all around, "this sure is a nice house."

"Ah . . . um, also my mother says I have to practice the piano, Barbara, so . . . ah, I guess you'd better go. I'm . . . I'm sorry."

Barbara gave me a sad look and left without another word. I didn't go back to the library for the rest of the summer.

Which is why I arranged to have Kat meet Teddy at his campus office.

As we crossed the Princeton campus, I chattered non-stop about my historic home town. In front of Nassau Hall, I stopped to say, "Did you know The Continental Congress met here in 1778? And that made Princeton the capital of the whole country for two weeks?"

Kat yawned behind her hand.

"See there's some bullet holes from the American Revolution." I pointed. This time Kat yawned and didn't bother covering her mouth.

"Gee, sorry I'm boring you so much," I said, biting each word off angrily.

"S'okay," Kat said, "I just don't go for old stuff."

I pointed to the bronze tigers in front of Nassau Hall. "See those? Touch them and you'll have good luck."

Kat limped over and rubbed one tiger's shiny nose.

Two guys in white sailor suits and black ties were rubbing the other tiger's nose.

"Oh boy, they're here," I said softly.

"Who?"

"The V-12s, Navy guys." I jumped up and down. "Oooh, that's so exciting!"

Kat gave me a cold look. "You think war's exciting?"

"Not exactly," I said. But in a way I did. I'd seen Movietone News about bombs dropping in faraway places, but the explosions didn't seem real. What I loved was rolling up the foil that came in Mum's cigarette packages and donating it to the Red Cross,

17

collecting newspapers and bacon grease and doing everything I could to help the war effort.

"If I were fifteen," I said, "I'd sign up to work at the campus canteen. The Upper School girls get to make sandwiches and give them out to servicemen." I turned to look at Kat. "Hey, you're fifteen. You could do it." Kat shrugged. "It's your patriotic duty," I snapped, "I'd do it if I could."

Kat sniffed. "You would. I wouldn't."

"I should think . . ." I said, then stopped.

Kat shifted her weight from one foot to the other. "Think what?"

"Oh nothing." But the words tumbled out of my mouth before I could stop them. "Teddy told me Jews are having a terrible time in Germany." Again I tried to stop, but the words kept coming, "Hitler's making them put on yellow armbands. You're Jewish. Doesn't that make you mad to hear that? Doesn't that make you want to win the war even more than me?"

Kat ran one hand through her curly hair. "Of course I want to win the war. Everybody does. But why do you keep harping on my being Jewish? In California, nobody talked about our religion. My family doesn't go to temple or anything. But in Princeton, people act like being Jewish means you smell bad."

I looked at my loafers, embarrassment flaming my face.

Kat went on, "David is obsessed with beating Hitler and Mom's worried sick about her cousins. That's why I want your grandfather to . . ."

I broke in, "Oh I remember. You're going to ask Teddy's friends to find your mother's cousins?"

Kat narrowed her eyes. "Don't you dare blab anything about that to the hair band girls."

"No, honest I won't."

We walked up the steps to Teddy's building. My grandfather was pretty absent minded. I hoped he remembered we were coming.

But when I knocked there was Teddy sitting behind his messy desk, smiling at us.

After introductions, my grandfather said to Kat, "Rosemary said you have questions for me?"

"Yes," Kat steadied herself on his desk, "but they're kind of private . . ."

"Rosemary, please wait outside," Teddy cleared books off a chair so Kat could sit. He winked at me. "Improve your mind by contemplating the beauties of nature."

I stormed downstairs. "Improve your mind. Oh really!" I sat down on the cold stone steps, still fuming.

"Rosemary." I saw a pair of shiny loafers and looked up. David Goodman, divinely handsome in a black sweater and khaki pants, stood over me. "Is my sister in there talking to your grandfather?"

I nodded. Being around David took my voice away.

He sat down beside me. "Kat says I should apologize for yelling at you. She said your grandfather's politics aren't your fault."

"It's h-his religion, not his politics," My heart was beating so loud I couldn't hear my own voice. "And it's a-all right about yelling. The whole town's mad at him."

Boys in my dancing class were repulsive. But David Goodman was gorgeous. Like Peter Lawford in *A Yank at Eton.*

He smiled. "I'm glad Kat's got one good friend."

"Ummm." I looked up in an elm tree where a squirrel sat on a branch nibbling a nut.

"She's had a rough two years. What with polio, and moving east and dealing with the snobs at your school. I told her to switch to the public high school where there are other Jewish kids, but she won't."

"Why?" I hoped he'd say it was because of me.

"She likes the science teacher," David said.

Awful Miss Stockbridge?

I was silent for a moment. Then I said, "Was it polio gave her the stiff leg?"

He nodded. "In bed for months. They weren't sure she'd walk again. But as you can see, she's okay—on that score at least."

"I think she's terrific," I lied, "I like her a lot."

"Really?" He studied my face. "My sister's an odd bird. Usually takes people a while to warm up to her."

"But I love people." I babbled. "Don't worry about Kat at our school. After I show her the ropes, she'll fit right in." A gloomy voice in my head said, *and when I get into Lucy's club, I don't think I can be Kat's friend any more.*

David stood, dusting off his pants. "It's a helluva assignment." Then he squatted down, his eyes level with mine. "Kat needs a loyal friend. It'll mean a lot to her if you stick by her. It'll mean a lot to me too."

I don't usually lie, but when I'm cornered, I can do it. Now, gazing into David Goodman's beautiful brown eyes, I said in my most sincere voice, "I promise I'll be a loyal friend to your sister."

"Atta girl." David patted my shoulder and loped off.

And I sat on the steps waiting for a bolt of lightning to strike me dead.

Saturday, April 11, 1942
RAF Runs Into Fierce Fight Over France,
Loses 4 Planes

Chapter Five

Saturday morning, Teddy invited some Quaker friends over. When they left, he put a metal clip around his pants leg and wheeled his black Raleigh bike out of the barn.

Mum called out, "It's going to rain."

Teddy glanced at the sky. "Grace, I need to clear my brain."

"Can I go with you?" I asked. He nodded. I yelled at Mum, "I'll watch out for him."

We pedaled along the country road where the air smelled of wet grass. The sky was as gray as Jackie's lead soldiers. I had loads of questions for Teddy, but didn't know how to start. Finally I cleared my throat and said, "Mrs. Lavalle hates what you say about the war."

"She and the rest of Princeton," Teddy said with a smile.

"Well, what do you expect?" I snapped. "It's wartime. We're supposed to be patriotic."

"I am doing what I think is right." He sighed.

"You hate this war, don't you?"

Looking sad, Teddy said, "World War I was supposed to be the war to end all wars. There was not supposed to be a World War II."

The wind rose and I had to shout. "This war is all Hitler's fault!" Teddy shook his head. "Yes it is. He's marching all over Europe. If we don't fight back, he'll take over the whole world."

"We Quakers think peace is the greater . . ." The wind snatched the end of his sentence.

Now I had to holler. "Even Einstein says we have to fight Hitler."

"Professor Einstein is a man of integrity. However," Teddy shouted back, eyes twinkling, "I think if Einstein was thy grandfather, he would embarrass thee as much as I do, with his bushy hair and no socks."

"It's not funny." The wind dropped and my voice boomed out too loud in the silence. "Mum's friends are treating her badly because of what you say."

"Is thee concerned about thy mother or thyself?"

I turned away from his bright eyes and mumbled, "The war's changed everything."

Teddy's voice was gentle. "Thee is growing. Growth means change and change is painful."

"It's the war that forced me to make friends with Kat Goodman."

Teddy looked surprised. "But she's a fine person."

"She's rude. She won't even tell me what you two talked about."

"Then neither will I," Teddy said.

"I can't ask her to your house. Because . . . well, because of Mum."

Teddy sighed. "Thee must be patient with thy mother."

Thunder rumbled far away. Drops splashed on the asphalt road.

"Uh oh," I pedaled faster. "Mum will kill us if we get wet."

We turned our bikes homeward. The raindrops made a silvery screen between Teddy and me. That gave me the courage to ask my grandfather some more questions.

"Daddy says it's important to have people like you. How come you don't care when people get mad at you?"

"Thy father is a good salesman. I am just a simple Quaker bearing witness to my beliefs."

"But Mum and Daddy keep telling me to go along with the crowd."

"If you listen to everyone," Teddy was pumping hard and he sounded out of breath, "how can you form your own ideas? Almost . . . home," he wheezed.

We slogged into the kitchen, dripping like fresh caught fish. Mum ran for towels. I shivered. Teddy coughed.

Mum said, "Oh Father, I hope this doesn't turn into pneumonia."

Teddy didn't get pneumonia, but he got a high fever and had to stay in bed for a week. Gas rationing began. Mum only qualified for an A sticker on her car, the one that gives you the least gas. Because of Teddy's illness, the Board gave us a temporary E sticker.

I stopped by Teddy's room after school. Mum carried a tray in and plunked it down on his bed. She looked at his white face and shivered.

"You don't look well, Father. Maybe you should go to the hospital."

"Don't fuss, Grace."

"Well, who has to nurse you?"

"I'll make sure he eats," I said as Mum left.

Teddy spooned up some canned vegetable soup. I spread greasy white margarine on his toast. Before the war nobody ate margarine, but real butter was now as scarce as gas.

After three bites, Teddy pushed the tray away. "I can't eat any more even to please thy mother. Poor Grace. Missing her husband makes her miserable."

What about me, I thought. Don't you think I miss my dad? But I bit the words back and glared at the wall.

"Ah Rosemary," Teddy said gently, "if thee wants to do something that will really help thy mother, thee could try entertaining Jackie."

I blushed, ashamed because I'd been thinking about myself, not about how I could help Mum. With a weary sigh, I picked up his tray.

"Guess what, Teddy?" I tried to sound cheerful. "Your sickness was an ill wind that blew us some good gas coupons. But when you're well, they'll take them away. We all might have to bike into town."

He coughed, then said, "Sufficient unto the day is the evil thereof."

Sometimes Teddy's patience drove me crazy. "But what if it's raining. The gas board will *have* to let you drive then. Else you could get sick and die!"

His lips twitched. "Ah Rosemary, what a flair thee has for drama."

I scowled. "Maybe you'd rather I was a scientist like Kat."

"I like you just the way you are." He coughed and closed his eyes.

In the kitchen, Jackie was making ack-ack noises as he pushed toy tanks and guns around the linoleum floor. His face was the color of rice pudding. To tell the truth he looked kind of pathetic.

I dumped the soup and bread into the garbage before Mum saw how much Teddy had eaten. Then I turned to Jackie, "Want to play Chinese checkers?"

He beamed. "Oh yeah. Sure." He raced to his room to get the board. "Yippee!" he yelled going down the hall, "bombs awaaaay!"

Mum lifted her head from a sinkful of dishes. "Rosemary, that's that nicest thing you could do for me. Thank you."

Teddy was such a wise man. If only he could tell me what to do about Lucy.

Last year, Lucy and I had so much fun. She'd come out here and we'd play with Teddy's kittens. We'd dress them in doll clothes and take them around the farm in the wheelbarrow. Last year we both wore overalls and braided our long hair. This year Lucy kept running her hands over her blonde pageboy and checking her face in her compact mirror. She and Mona were best friends now. They talked about boys all day long. Daddy said I'd be back in their crowd as soon as I got interested in boys. He could be right. But why did being boy crazy make Lucy so mean to Kat?

Yesterday, she'd asked if anyone had a swimming pool we could use for the class party. Nobody volunteered. She kept asking. Finally Kat said, "Guess you could use ours."

Lucy's eyes and mouth went huge. "Yours?" She shook her head. "No, I don't think so."

"What's wrong with our pool?" Kat asked scowling.

Lucy tipped her nose into the air. "My mother doesn't let me go to places where she's not sure the pool is clean."

Kat tried to look as if she didn't care, but her hands trembled as she jammed them into her skirt pockets. I wanted to ask Lucy if she didn't like Kat, why didn't she just leave her alone?

Then I remembered how Lucy used to take a long time getting used to new things. In middle school when we started moving from one class to another, the first week she got all confused and burst into tears. Soon she was comfortable with the new routine. Maybe when she gets used to Kat, she'll act nicer. Maybe.

Friday, April 17, 1942
More German Gestapo Sent to Italy
Hitler-Mussolini Meeting

Chapter Six

Friday night, Mum asked if I wanted to go to Mrs. Wainwright's with her. "She's having a party."

"No thanks," I said really fast, hurrying to my room.

Mrs. Wainwright was an awful woman with dyed red hair. Whenever I got within two feet of her, she'd grab me and croon, "Daaahling". Her breath smelled of gin.

"Lucy's going to be there," Mum said.

I stopped halfway up the stairs. "Okay, I'll go. But I've outgrown last year's party dress. What can I wear?"

Mum rummaged in her closet and put together an outfit. It was different, but I thought I looked good. Maybe tonight, I thought, hopping from foot to foot, if Mona doesn't come, Lucy and I will get buddy-buddy.

Mrs. Wainwright lived on Mercer Street around the corner from our old house. Mum parked in front of Einstein's house. She lit a cigarette, but didn't open the car door.

"Think she's invited Professor Einstein?" I asked.

Mum shook her head. "And even if she asked him, he wouldn't come."

"How do you know?"

"He says parties are a waste of time."

"Well, he goes to some parties. He played his violin for the British War Relief."

"Rosemary, please stop talking and let me think."

"About what?"

"Gas rationing. Father won't ask for more gas. And he refuses to move. How are we going to get you two to school and him to his classes?"

"Jackie doesn't care if he never goes to school. And Teddy and I," I said, "can bike into town."

"Honestly," Mum puffed on her Chesterfield. "Do you really think your grandfather can bike to work through rain and snow?"

I giggled, imagining my bony grandfather pedaling through a snowstorm, his striped tie flying out behind and his tweed jacket flapping. He'd look like Ichabod Crane.

"It's not funny. I've spent my whole life being embarrassed by what my father does."

"You mean like not believing in war?"

Mum stubbed out her cigarette fiercely, "That and a lot of other things. When I was growing up, everybody in town had a maid. Except us. We had the money to hire one, but Father convinced Mother he could do all our cooking. I could never bring my friends home for meals. You've eaten Teddy's food. You understand."

"His cooking is pretty bad," I admitted. "Mum, why doesn't Teddy care what people think?"

Mum sighed and opened the car door. "Maybe because he's an intellectual, like Professor Einstein. But ordinary people like us can't be so fancy. We have to go along with the crowd."

"I'm trying," I said in a small voice. Mum patted my shoulder.

Mrs. Wainwright's living room was jammed. A man with lots of dark hair sat on the piano bench. Lucy Lavalle stood near him.

I bounced up to her. "Hi Lucy, you look cute." She was wearing an off the shoulder cotton dress with pink and blue flowers, a pink velvet hair band and baby doll shoes.

Lucy looked me over, eyes narrowed. "Is that your mother's blouse?"

Mum had loaned me a white linen blouse with a sailor collar which I wore with my navy blue skirt. She'd braided my curly hair and wound the plaits around my head. "Tres chic," she said and I felt fine until this minute. Lucy's X-ray stare was draining my confidence.

Lucy hissed just like Mona, then she whirled around. "Have you seen that sensational number?"

"Where?"

"Over there." She pointed to a boy about our age with dark hair and pimples. He was Lucy's height and his tie looked like it was choking him.

"The guy with the spots?"

"Rosemary, you are soooo superficial." Lucy did her eyebrow thing. "He's French. I'm dying to meet him." She wove through the crowd toward the boy.

Suddenly I heard Mrs. Wainwright's trumpet voice call, "Oh my daaahling child!" She was steaming toward me, purple scarves fluttering and the smell of gin stinking up the air. "Come here to me . . ."

I backed away from her, pushed on the nearest door and found myself in the kitchen. I crouched under the table in the breakfast nook hoping she wouldn't think to look there. I waited, but nobody came into the kitchen, thank God. Finally I dared raise my head to look around.

The kitchen smelled sour. The pile of dishes in the sink crawled with flies. A big table in the middle of the room was loaded with wax paper covered platters—sandwiches, stuffed eggs, and a huge roasted turkey.

Meat. My mouth watered. I walked to the table, put out one finger and touched its crispy skin. My finger came away covered with hair. Red hair. Ugh. I stepped back, slipped on something greasy and fell on my behind. "Damn!"

As if on signal, a big red dog bounded in, put its paws on the table and wrestled the turkey down on top of me.

"Stop that!" I kicked at the dog. "Get off me!"

Someone said, "*Merde*, you've done it again!"

"I didn't do anything," I shouted.

"Not you. Fiona." It was the spotty boy. He picked the turkey up and put it back on the platter. "That's the third time she has done that." He had a foreign accent, but his English was good.

I shuddered. "Nobody can eat that turkey now."

He shrugged. "It's not poison. Just covered with dog hair." He shoved Fiona outside and slammed the door.

"I wouldn't eat hairy turkey for a million dollars."

"Americans," he said, "don't know nothing about hunger. If you were starving, you'd feel different." He took out a package of cigarettes and lit one. I stared. How old was this boy anyhow? Twin plumes of smoke came out of his nostrils. "Once I ate only raw turnips for two days."

I swallowed. I'd never heard anybody talk about starving. "Your English is good," I said.

"My mother was American." His eyes had the shiny look that meant tears were near.

Careful, Rosemary. "Um . . . when did you leave France?"

"Six months now, I have escaped with my father."

And where is your mother? "H-how did you escape?"

"I don't talk about that." He clenched both hands into tight fists.

So what's a safe question? "Where do you go to school?"

"Lawrenceville. I am sophomore."

"Is your father here too?"

"At this party? *Bien sur.* You think I'd come of my own will?" He paced the floor, pulling smoke into his lungs, then coughing as if he hadn't been smoking long.

As he walked past the turkey, he said, "That meat smelled very delicious when Agnes was roasting it. She was a very good cook. But Madame Wainwright was rude to her and Agnes put on her hat and her coat and left."

"Well, if the maid's quit, maybe we should pass around some of this food. Not the turkey, of course."

He ground his cigarette out on the floor. "Me, I don't go out there."

"Why? Does Mrs. Wainwright grab you like she does me?"

"Not if I see her first." His grin was nice. His nose turned up at the end and his teeth were small and white. He put his hand under the wax paper and grabbed two sandwiches.

I grinned back. "I came in here to escape her." He laughed. Encouraged, I went on, "Everybody says she has bad manners because she used to be a waitress before she married Mr. Wainwright."

His smile died. "Oh. Is that what you Americans call small talk?" He sniffed. "Of course, this is a small town."

I stiffened. "Princeton's a wonderful town," I shot back. "Our university is famous and lots of famous people live here. So there!"

"I am from Paris," he drawled, "the world's most cosmopolitan city."

I felt like punching him. "What did your father do before the war?"

He stared. "You have not heard of my father?"

"How could I have heard of him if I never met him?"

"He . . ."

"Yves, where are you? Yves!" Mrs. Wainwright's loud voice could shatter windows.

"*Merde*," said the boy and pushed the door open. I followed him into the living room.

Mrs. Wainwright stood beside the grand piano. She rested one hand on the shoulder of the dark haired man who was sitting on the piano bench. Raising her voice and waving her scarves, she said, "You've all met my fiancé, the famous pianist Claude Galoupe. This is his adorable son." Beckoning. "Come here, Yves, my little love." She beckoned. Yves took a step backward, a grim look on his face.

I gasped. *Her fiancé?* So Yves' dad was marrying Mrs. W? I wanted to run back to the kitchen. No wonder he didn't like me making catty remarks about how she had no manners. No wonder he got mad. I wished I could take back what I said.

I looked up. Yves was grinning at me. Mrs. Wainwright took his arm. He crossed his eyes. I smiled at him.

Suddenly Lucy was at my elbow. "Why's he making faces at you?" She shook my arm. "Where did you go?"

"I . . ."

"Where *were* you?"

"In the kitchen. This dog pulled a turkey off the table and then Yves shooed the dog off me and . . ."

Lucy frowned. "Tell me what really happened," she demanded.

30

"I just *told* you. And Lucy, don't eat the turkey. I tried to brush off the dog hair, but . . ."

Lucy's eyes sparked. "You're making fun of me." She flounced off smoothing her hair. Sense of humor had never been Lucy's strong point.

I went to find Mum who was sitting on a window seat next to Lucy's mother.

As I came up, Mrs. Lavalle said, "Why Miss Sowerby is willing to mix the races at her school, I'll never know."

Mum twisted her cocktail glass in her thin fingers. "I don't know what to say to Rosemary . . ."

"Tell her what I told my Lucy. Actually," Mrs. Lavalle tittered, "Lucy and I have a little code which we use when we're talking about people like that. We say that girl is NOKD. It means Not Our Kind Dear."

Wow. So that's where Lucy got her razor tongue. I tugged on Mum's sleeve, "Can we go home now?"

"Oh." Mum's face was pink. "We were just talking about . . ."

". . . you girls," said Mrs. Lavalle.

Mum put down her glass and started for the door. I followed her, feeling angry all the way through. NOKD, my foot. What would Mrs. Lavalle say if I told her that her precious Lucy was the one forcing me to make friends with Kat Goodman?

When we got into the car, I was still angry. "Mum, why does everyone hate Jews?"

"I'm sorry you heard what Peggy Lavalle said," Mum sounded embarrassed. "Gladys Wainwright serves too much booze at her parties and not enough food. Everyone gets pie-eyed and it makes them talk too much."

I nodded, but to myself I thought Mrs. Lavalle would say mean things about Kat even if she hadn't been drinking. And when she talked about NOKD, Mum didn't say a word. Like tell her that was a really mean thing to say. But I knew that she believed you had to go along with people even when they said awful things. Nobody was brave enough to speak up except Teddy.

I shivered. What if Teddy found out that I was only trying to make friends with Kat as an initiation stunt to get into Lucy's club? What would he think of me then?

As Mum drove home, I stared out into the dark wondering what it was like to eat nothing but raw turnips for two days.

Monday, April 20, 1942
Corregidor Surrenders
British Hit Madagascar

Chapter Seven

Monday, as I climbed up the school steps, one of Lucy's henchmen stopped me. "Mona wants to see you," she said, "in the cloakroom."

Mona wants to see me? I passed three more girls who said the same thing. In the cloakroom, I hung up my sweater, then turned to face Mona. "You were looking for me?"

"Yes, Rosemary." Mona's whispery voice made mine sound like a braying donkey. Her shiny brown hair was folded into a hairnet and her gathered dirndl skirt showed off her tiny waist.

I took out a brush and tried to untangle my curls. Mona nudged me toward the bathroom. "Rosemary, I feel terrible about what she's making you do."

"What do you mean?"

"Lucy. Forcing you to hang around with that awful Jewish girl." Small hiss.

I turned to stare at her. "I thought it was your idea."

"I'll admit," Mona looked down at her tiny little toes. "I *did* think you were too young to be a member of our club, but when I heard the French boy was paying attention to you at the party . . ." her silly smile reminded me of a stupid wooden doll I gave away years ago.

Mona stood on tiptoe and breathed into my ear, "Lucy likes that French boy. But if you want to cut her out, I'll show you how."

"Button your lip, Pee Wee." My voice was hoarse. "I'm not interested in cutting Lucy out of anything and I think it's rotten of you to talk behind her back."

"Atta girl!" The toilet door slammed and out came Lucy. "See Mona, I told you she was loyal."

Barely breathing, I looked from one to the other. "That was a dirty trick you just played on me."

"Mona wanted to test you," Lucy's cheeks were red, and her eyes slid past my face to look out the window, "and you passed her test with an A plus. I knew you would, Rosie."

I gripped my books so tight the corners dug into my ribs as I looked at my oldest friend. I wasn't crying. The only reason there were tears in my eyes was because the books hurt my ribs. I'd been eager to get into the club, to be part of the popular group in my class. I thought if I was a club member everyone would be nice to me. Now I wasn't so sure.

Our first class was English. Our teacher, Mrs. Hazeltine, had ink blue circles under her eyes. Probably worried about her husband. The news from the Pacific was terrible. The Japs were sinking our battleships and attacking Bataan. Even Movietone News couldn't make it sound good.

"Today we'll read from Shakespeare's Henry the Fifth," Mrs. Hazeltine said. She told us each to choose the speech we wanted to do.

Mrs. Hazeltine picked three girls to read. Then she said, "You'll read fourth, Rosemary."

The other girls droned their lines as if they were trying to put us to sleep.

When it was my turn, I stood up, clutching the book.

"Once more unto the breach," I said and threw all my hurt feelings into the speech that Prince Henry gave his soldiers before a big fight. When I said "mean and base" I shot a dirty look at Lucy and Mona. At the end I raised my fist in the air and cried, "Cry—God for Harry! England! and St. Geeeooorge!"

Someone tittered.

"Quiet!" Mrs. Hazeltine said. "If everyone put as much spirit into their speech as Rosemary Hoyt just did, you'd all be getting As."

At the end of the period, Mrs. Hazeltine beckoned me up to her desk. "That was stirring, Rosemary. You should recite that speech for the War Relief Assembly. You'd make the whole school want to enlist."

I smiled, but I was still angry as I left class. In the hall, I saw Kat leaning against the wall.

She said, "Want to eat lunch in the lab?"

I shook my head. My stomach was churning.

Kat limped beside me as I marched down the hall. "David says I've got to quit being so standoffish."

David! My hand flew to my mouth. I'd forgotten my promise to him. "Okay," I said, "I'll eat with you if you tell me what you talked to my grandfather about."

"He didn't tell you?" I shook my head. "I don't get that old guy," Kat said, "he's ixnay on the war, but he helps smuggle Jews out of Germany. It doesn't make sense."

"It does if you're a Quaker," I told her, "they don't believe in war, but they believe in goodness and in helping people."

We were standing in the middle of the hall. Girls were streaming around us. Someone said in a low voice, "Hey yid, quit hogging the hall." I wheeled, but couldn't spot who had the nasty mouth.

Kat pretended she hadn't heard. "So will you come to the lab for lunch?"

"Yes."

We sat at a black counter facing a row of Bunsen burners. Over in the corner, Miss Stockbridge was washing a sink full of glass tubes. She nodded to us.

Kat opened her paper bag and pulled out a wrapped package. "Louis' wife made crepes today. Want one?"

I peered at a bunch of things that looked like fat gray pillows. "Uh . . . no . . . no thanks. I've got cream cheese and jelly."

Kat asked, "Did you listen to Charlie McCarthy last night?"

"Nope. Teddy only turns his radio on for the Philharmonic and the opera."

"Whew, this town sure is full of highbrows." A smile twisted Kat's wide mouth.

"I'm dying to get a radio," I admitted. "I want to listen to the Hit Parade. But Mum says Daddy's Navy pay doesn't stretch to buying extras." *Uh oh. I shouldn't have admitted that we were poor. Now Lucy says Kat will start boasting that her family is rich.*

But Kat didn't say a word. She was busily biting into her crepe. Suddenly, brown juice squirted all over her bright green dress. Cursing, she dabbed at the stain with a paper napkin. "Mom's going to murder me. She just bought this stupid dress." She wet her napkin and scrubbed until the outline of her bra showed under the damp material. I watched wide-eyed.

"That's why I like science," Kat said, "follow the rules and your experiment always comes out right."

"Boring," I replied. Who wanted things to be the same every time?

Kat shrugged her shoulders into a white lab coat. "I'm going to show you something."

She lined up: a beaker, a piece of wire, a glass bottle. Then asked Miss Stockbridge a question. The teacher nodded.

Kat returned. "In this beaker I put five grams of pure copper wire. Now I'll add . . ." she looked at a sheet of paper, "four milliliters of concentrated nitric acid." Carefully she poured from the bottle into the beaker. She lit the Bunsen burner and fixed an upside down funnel over it, then inserted a glass tube into the funnel opening and pointed the tube at the wall.

I inched closer, the heat of the flame warming my face. Orangey brown stuff swirled around in the beaker, then rose in the air. I stretched out my forefinger to see if it was warm.

"Get away from that!" Kat yelled.

I jumped. My hand hit the funnel. The glass tube broke. A cloud of stinking gas puffed into the air.

"Fyew, fyew!" I pinched my nose.

"Don't breathe that stuff!" Kat pushed me back against the wall. Miss Stockbridge got up and turned off the burner. Kat apologized then turned to me. "Did you do that on purpose?"

"Of course not."

Miss Stockbridge picked up the beaker with a pair of tongs and dropped it into the sink. She handed Kat a rag. Kat began cleaning the counter.

Nervous giggles bubbled out of my throat. "S-sorry . . . what did I ruin?"

"Acid base neutralization. An experiment that never fails."

"Oh yeah?" I laughed.

After a minute, Kat joined in. "Help me clean this up."

We worked in silence. When the mess was cleaned up, Kat said, "Chemistry is easier for me than people. I've done that experiment a ton of times and it always comes out okay. Then I involve just one person and . . ."

"Hey, I said I was sorry. Don't rub it in."

"I wasn't rubbing it in. Just saying that science is a lot more reliable than people."

I squirmed, a guilty conscience twisting my stomach. "I think most people want to be nice . . ."

"They do if it's easy," Kat said.

I looked down at the counter in silence.

"My mother," Kat said, "is begging me to ask a friend to our house. If I admit I don't have any friends at this school, she'll force me to switch to Princeton High School."

"David said you might be better off there."

"David," Kat said, "is an emotional type. I'm a rational person."

I thought about getting emotional with David Goodman and my breathing stopped.

Kat waggled her finger. "Jeeze, all my brother has to do is wave his eyelashes and every girl in sight comes running."

I shot to my feet, face burning, and gathered up my books.

"So will you come home with me tomorrow?" Kat asked.

I stopped, feeling torn. I'd promised David I'd be a good friend to Kat. What's more, a trip to Kat's house would show Lucy I was getting buddy-buddy with Kat like I was supposed to. But what if I got into Lucy's club and those girls said I couldn't talk to Kat any more? What would David Goodman say about me then? What would Teddy say? What would I say about myself?

"So will you come?" Kat repeated, "just this once?"

"Okay," I said.

Tuesday, April 24, 1942
Great Naval and Air Battles In The Pacific
Gas Rationing: 2-3 Gallons a Week

Chapter Eight

As usual Mum sat down at the table with one finger holding her place in a book. When she picked up her fork and started reading, I mumbled that I was going to visit someone after school and would get my own ride home. Mum nodded and turned the page, not really paying attention.

The next day I went to school all ready to go visit the Goodmans. But Kat was absent.

"I bet it's Passout," Lucy whispered as she hung up her sweater, "that's a Jewish holiday."

Another club girl said, "My father says Wall Street's almost empty during Passout."

"Passover, you dopes," I yanked a comb through my curls. "Lucy, don't you remember in Sunday School when they told us about Egypt and the angel writing on the Jewish people's doors to keep them safe?" Lucy shook her head. "Anyway, Kat wouldn't skip school because of a Jewish holiday. She's not religious. Neither is her family."

Lucy looked at Mona, then said, "It's Wednesday, Rosie, want to eat with us in Renwick's?"

Oh wow. "You mean I'm getting into your club?"

"Soon," Lucy sounded sincere. "So do you want to eat with us?"

"Oh, yes. Golly, yes!"

The girls in the club filled up two booths in Renwick's. I was squashed in between Lucy and Mona. My armpits felt wet and I hoped I didn't have B.O.

Everybody ordered cokes and no food because they were all on diets. My stomach growled. But even with a dollar in my pocket, I didn't dare order a hamburger. It felt great though, sitting with all my old friends, being part of their group.

A boy walked by. Lucy flipped her pageboy back. "What a dreamboat."

Mona sang, "Your dreams are getting better all the time." Everybody laughed. Mona went on, "Lawrenceville is sending a busload of boys into town this afternoon. Bill told me he'd be on it."

I looked at her. "Who's Bill?" Nobody answered.

Mona leaned across me to talk to Lucy. "What about that French boy you met? Is he coming on the bus?"

Lucy looked as if she'd bitten into a crab apple. "Not sure."

"Yves?" I said, "I thought he lived in Mrs. Wainwright's house."

"He's moved to Lawrenceville because his father's on tour," Lucy told me, "and Yves can't stand living with Mrs. W." She stopped, then her eyes got big, "Oh, here comes DTGJ."

I turned. David Goodman was at the counter getting an ice cream cone.

On his way out, he stopped at my booth. "Hi, Rosemary." He gave me the once-over. "You eating with the 'in' group at Miss Worth's?"

Big silence. Finally I found my voice. "Kat's absent today. Is she sick?"

"She didn't tell you?" He licked through chocolate jimmies to reach his white ice cream.

"No, but she invited me to her house, so I wondered . . ."

"Guess she'd tell you, if she wanted you to know." He strode away.

Mona put her face too close to mine. "David's got the hots for you, David's got the hots for you."

I bent over my coke. "What does DTGJ mean?"

"Need you ask?" Mona hissed.

"I'm asking." I stirred my coke until ice chips flew into the air.

"It's our secret code." Mona tucked her hair behind her small ears with a kitty cat smile.

I felt my temper rise. "Can't anyone answer a simple question?"

"If you must know," Mona said primly, "DTGJ stands for David, The Gorgeous Jew."

I shot out of my seat. "That's disgusting!"

Lucy looked rattled. "Remember about sticks and stones, Rosie. Remember that names won't hurt him. Sit down."

I pushed my way out of the booth.

"Where are you going?" Lucy asked.

"I'm going to the movies. Here's a dime for my coke. And if you don't like it, you can lump it."

Lucy gave Mona her eyebrow routine. Then, "Hey group, why don't we all take in a flick?"

"But I'm supposed to meet Bill here." Mona whined.

The others got up and filed out behind Lucy. Mona followed, a pouting expression on her face.

We walked through Palmer Square to the Playhouse Theater. One of the mousiest girls in the club sidled up to me.

She whispered, "That was a horrible thing to say. But you have to go along with them. Otherwise they blackball you and you don't have any friends."

We filled up the back row of the movie theater. The newsreel showed Bugs Bunny selling War Bonds and shots of soldiers fighting in Africa. The sound of gunfire banged around inside my head.

The feature began. It was about France and some British fliers trying to escape the Nazis who were occupying the country. The Nazis were hunting for the fliers. Like they hunted Yves and his family.

Somebody passed around a box of Good and Plentys. I crammed some in my mouth, still staring at the screen.

I thought about Kat. Lunch in the science lab with her was more fun than I expected. After I ruined her experiment, we'd had a big laugh. I hadn't laughed that hard in a long time. What I'd really like was to join Lucy's club and still stay friends with Kat. But I was afraid I'd have to choose. The Club or Kat? I know what Mum would say. "Stick with the people who count." I knew what Teddy would say. But what would *I* choose?

Lucy leaned close. "Did I hear you say Kat invited you to go over to her house?"

"Quiet," said a woman in front.

Lucy spoke very softly. "You have to go. And report back to us. After that, you'll definitely be in our club."

I rubbed my stomach where the Good and Plentys were starting to make me feel sick.

Monday, April 27, 1942
10,000 Prisoners in Manila Bay Forts
40 French Hostages Shot in Occupied France

Chapter Nine

Kat didn't return to school for three days. During that time, the club girls pestered me with detailed instructions on what to do when I finally got to her house.

Mona. "Find out how much money the Goodmans have."

I gasped. "I can't ask her that. It's rude to talk about money."

"Jews like to talk about money," Lucy said grimly, "My dad says so."

Mona said, "Our maid used to work for some Jews. She says they aren't allowed to eat meat and milk at the same meal."

"So what?" I said.

"Watch your mouth," Mona shot back, hands on her hips.

I felt trapped. "Look, couldn't we just forget about me making friends with Kat? What if instead of that I asked Albert Einstein to come and play his violin at our War Relief Assembly? That would take a lot of nerve. Inviting him to come, I mean."

"Rosemary," Mona broke in, "stop babbling about Albert Einstein." She looked at me through slitted eyes. "Find out if the Goodmans use the black market. See if they chisel extra gas. My mother says all Jews do that."

"I thought I was supposed to make *friends* with Kat. You didn't tell me I had to *spy* on her."

They stared at me. Mona hissed. Lucy shook her head sadly. Arm in arm, they walked away.

The Goodman limousine was lined with gray upholstery and smelled like cigars. There was a glass window between the chauffeur and us, just like in the movies.

Kat noticed me staring. "In case you're wondering how we get the gas, it's because my Dad does essential war work."

I happened to know Mr. Goodman took the train to New York. So I bet the extra gas was because of Kat's leg. "Where did you go last week?"

Kat pursed her lips. "David saw you in Renwick's with the hair band snobs."

I leaned back on the soft seat. "You were gone. Who else was there to eat with?"

Kat hesitated. "Mom dragged me to a lot of stupid doctors in New York and Baltimore." She grimaced. "She won't quit until somebody guarantees that I'll be dancing next year." She made a face.

"What's wrong with that?"

"I don't want to dance," Kat rummaged in her purse. "Hey, I bought you something in New York." She pulled out a blue knitted bag with blue velvet ribbons dangling from it.

I stared. "What is it?"

"A snood. You stuff your hair in it. They're all the rage in Hollywood."

"Gee thanks. Did you get one for yourself?"

Kat shook her head. "I like my hair bushy. Like Albert Einstein. He's my hero. So what happened while I was gone?"

I didn't want Kat to know what the "hair band snobs" were saying about her so I told the story about the Wainwright party and the hairy turkey.

Kat chuckled. "You're a character, Rosemary. So's your grandfather."

"Have the Quakers located your mother's cousins?"

Kat looked out the window. "Did your grandfather get over his cold?"

So she wasn't going to answer me. What was the big secret about Teddy and those cousins?

The car drove through stone gateposts and up a long driveway. The Goodman house looked like Tara in *Gone with the Wind.* Inside, it reminded me of a house I'd seen in movies—black and white tiles on the floor, red silk draperies and a white piano.

"Wow, this place must have cost a fortune."

Kat looked surprised, "I dunno. Daddy said he grabbed it because it doesn't have any neighbors to make a stink about living next to Jews."

I blushed, deeply ashamed of the people in my town.

As we went inside, Kat called out, "Mom, where are you?"

A short dark haired woman wearing a uniform glided up to Kat and murmured in her ear.

"Oh darn it. Mom's gone to New York." Kat grinned, "Just when I wanted to prove to her I really did have a friend. Felice says she'll make us extra good snacks."

She limped around the first floor showing me all the rooms. I goggled at all the beautiful stuff—dark oil paintings and polished silver. Patterned rugs and huge couches. In the den there was a huge wooden box about three feet tall with a small glass panel set in the top. When Kat pressed a button, I could see fuzzy gray figures moving around. They looked like dancing dust balls.

"What's this?" I squinted at the glass.

"Television. That's a baseball game," Kat said, "Dad says television is going to be big. He wants to invest in it."

"How much?" I was desperate for a dollar figure I could pass on to Lucy.

Kat shrugged. "Dad never talks about money. Lately he hardly talks at all. He just goes around saying 'loose lips sink ships.'"

She led the way upstairs. Her bedroom was dreamy. A four poster bed with ruffled green and white curtains, a dressing table with a ruffled skirt. Lucy would die of envy.

Kat opened a bulging closet and pulled out a pink and white taffeta dress. "A date dress Mom bought me. Fat chance I'll ever get to wear it."

44

I peeked into the closet. "You've got some really nice clothes. Why do you wear the same baggy skirt and sweaters all the time?"

"I used to care what I looked like. You know… before . . ." she shrugged, "but now . . ." she pointed to her chemistry book. "I got better things to do than think about my outfits."

"Hey, people don't notice your leg."

Kat gave me a long look. "You kidding?"

"Well," I muttered, "at least you have breasts."

I sat down at Kat's dressing table and stuffed my hair into the new snood, then turned around smiling, "Think I look more like Loretta Young or Dorothy Lamour?"

Kat snickered. "More like Little Orphan Annie!"

My smile died. "I can't help it that I skipped a grade. I'm almost fourteen."

"Calm down, calm down. Want to see the rest of the upstairs?"

In Kat's parents' bedroom, there was a photograph in a heavy silver frame of a rugged man with his arm around a beautiful woman.

"Mom and Dad." Kat said. She pointed to another frame. "That's Mom with her Berlin cousins." Three smiling teenagers in fur coats and old fashioned hats. "They're the ones the Quakers are looking for."

"So you did ask Teddy to find them."

Kat hummed and tapped her fingers on the bureau. I picked up another frame. "Who's this?" A tanned girl in white shorts holding a tennis trophy.

"Me," Kat turned the picture face down. "Last tournament I'll be in."

I picked up the last photo. "Clark Gable!" I squealed. He was smiling down on a tiny girl. "Jeepers, is that you?"

"Yep. He's a family pal."

Wow! Clark Gable, the number one heartthrob at Miss Worth's. Lucy's idol And Kat's family knew him.

Then my eyes turned to the velvet cushion on a big window seat. It was piled high with packages of nylons, Hershey bars and cigarette cartons—Chesterfields, Lucky Strikes and Pall Malls.

Last week Mum stood in line for an hour to get just one carton of Chesterfields. Chocolate was really scarce and as for nylons, they were so hard to find women drew black lines on the back of their bare legs with eyebrow pencil so it would look like a stocking seam. Where did all this stuff come from?

"Do you want some candy? Take some," Kat waved one hand at the pile. I swallowed and shook my head. Much as I loved chocolate, I wasn't going to take anything. "Go ahead," she said, "grab some Hershey's. Dad brings home tons."

Tons. Did that mean he was using the black market? How else could he get those things? I wished we'd never come into this room, wished I'd never seen that window seat.

The maid came to the door. "I have put food in your room, Miss Kat."

Kat limped toward the door. "Let's eat."

On her bed was a big tray covered with iced cakes and tiny sandwiches, the kind Mum used to make for parties before the war.

I was still worried about the cigarettes, nylons and candy bars, but I popped a sandwich in my mouth. "Yummm. Delicious."

"Crab," Kat said. I took another

From the hall came a high pitched voice. "Enid, I need to speak to you. Alone!"

Kat made a face. "Uh oh. Mom's back. And having one of her nervous headaches, it sounds like." She went to the door. "Mom, I've got a school friend here."

"Come out here this instant."

Kat rolled her eyes and left the room, shutting the door behind her. I heard whispering.

Mrs. Goodman's voice rose to a scream, "It's terrible, terrible. They are like . . . no, I can't talk until that girl is gone. Call Louis to take her home."

Now I knew how Barbara Gates felt when Mum pulled me into the kitchen to tell me to send her home.

Kat returned, "Sorry." She ran her hands through her curls. "My mother's got an awful headache."

I stood up, pulling the snood off and stuffing it in my pocket. "I'm on my way."

Kat walked downstairs with me. "Sorry," she said again.

"I had a nice time." I knew I sounded stiff, but that's how I felt.

"You don't sound like you had a nice time."

Louis opened the door of the limousine.

46

"I can't help how I sound," I said crossly, climbing into the back seat.

Kat put her head in the window. "Don't be mad."

"I'm not."

"Come again?"

"Sure."

As Louis drove away, I chewed on my thumbnail. The crab sandwiches felt like rocks in my stomach.

If Lucy got the slightest hint that the Goodmans were using the black market, she'd pounce on it like a kitten pouncing on a ball of string. She wouldn't stop giving me the third degree until she'd wormed every last detail about those chocolates, nylons and cigarettes out of me. She'd say that proved that all Jews use the black market. She'd pass the word around school. People would act even meaner to Kat than they already did.

I laced my fingers together, then unlaced them. I cracked my knuckles and pressed my teeth into my lower lip. I'd promised David to be Kat's loyal friend and I wanted to keep my promise. But Lucy always had a sixth sense about when I was lying. If I acted the least bit different, she'd come at me over and over with questions. Could I hold out?

Wednesday, April 29, 1942
Axis Submarine in Gulf of Mexico,
Sunk 2 Boats

Chapter Ten

I didn't sleep well that night. The next morning my throat felt
like sandpaper. Good, I thought, I can stay home and practice
zipping my lip before I have to answer Lucy and Mona's questions.
I need time to think of some way to keep them for finding out what I
saw at the Goodmans.

At breakfast, I stuck out my tongue. "My mouth feels like the
bottom of a birdcage." Something my parents sometimes said after a
party.

"Me too, I feel sick too," Jackie said.

Mum looked us over. "You don't look well, either of you." She
tilted her head and sighed. "All right. You can stay home today. It'll
save one day's gas."

Jackie and I cheered.

The spring sun was warm. I played Chinese checkers with Jackie
at the picnic table, while Mum read a mystery. She boiled hot dogs
for lunch. Eating meat made it feel like a holiday.

After lunch, Mum started brushing my hair. "Such a mop! Maybe
we should cut it."

A formation of airplanes roared overhead.

"Achtung, achtung, American planes at twelve o clock, ack ack ack ack," yelled Jackie, pretending to shoot them.

"They are B-29s," said Mum who had memorized every American plane so she could be an air spotter for three hours a week. She went to the golf course with her binoculars and stared up at the sky watching for enemy planes. "And stop that German talk, Jackie or I'll have Dr. Fenton give you an enema."

"You should," I said. "He's sick in the head."

Jackie stuck out his lip. "You're not the boss of me."

Mum said, "Want me to braid your hair, Rosemary?"

"Sure, but hey, I've got something even better." I ran upstairs, and got out the snood Kat had given me. I stuffed my hair into it. Downstairs, I turned around in front of Mum. "Isn't it snazzy? It's called a snood."

"Where did you get it?"

"Kat Goodman bought it for me in New York." I twirled, hands on my hips. "All the Hollywood stars are wearing them."

Mum tightened her lips to a thin line. "But you are not a Hollywood star." After a pause, she went on, "Is that where you went yesterday? To the Jewish girl's house?"

I balled my hands into fists and squeezed, trying not to lose my temper. "Her name is Kat, Mum, not the Jewish girl."

"Did I give you permission to visit her?"

"I told you I was going." I stuck out my chin.

"If you say so." Mum rubbed her forehead. "I can't seem to remember things well these days."

Now I felt guilty. "Maybe *you* are the one who needs to go to the doctor."

"There's nothing really wrong with me. It's just so difficult with your father away . . ." Mum's voice trailed off and she sighed a deep sigh.

I noticed she had new lines crossing her forehead and deep ones between her eyes. I patted her hand and took off the snood. I lay back in the canvas deck chair while she braided my hair. The sun was warm on my face. I relaxed.

"Why, Rosemary," Mum's voice seemed to come from far away, "I hadn't noticed how big your breasts have grown."

"What!" I jerked upright.

"We'll have to buy you some bras," she said. I grabbed a towel and covered myself. "Don't be upset," Mum was smiling, "it's natural for a girl your age to develop."

I looked down and saw twin bumps showing under my knit shirt. Though I'd wanted breasts for ages, I didn't like the way they'd snuck up on me.

"Telephone, Rosemary," Jackie called from inside the house. "It's Lucy."

"Tell her I can't talk," I called back. "Sore throat."

"Baloney," he yelled.

I jumped up. "Tell her I'm sick or I'll strangle you."

"Okay, okay."

"Why Rosemary, what's wrong with you?" Mum was frowning now. "You're willing to go visit some Jewish girl you hardly know, but you won't talk to your best friend."

"My so-called best friend," my voice wobbled, but I tried not to cry, "treats me like a dog."

"There must be a reason for Lucy to cut you out. What did you do to her?"

My temper boiled over. "It's not what I did. It's what *she's* doing!" I yelled.

I ran for my bike and pedaled down the road toward Stony Brook. I cycled with my head down, tears dripping off my chin. I stuck my tongue out at a black and white cow. When I got to the stone bridge, I flung down my bike and slithered down the muddy bank. I took off my shoes and socks and waded into the shallow stream.

Before Lucy got boy crazy, the two of us used to come here a lot. We'd put our cheese sandwiches on a rock to "toast" and splash around in the cold water.

Today, the frosty water swirled around my ankles turning them blue. I picked up a flat stone and tried to skip it. A small stone plopped into the water beside me.

"Hey, cut that out!" I shouted, looking up at the bridge.

A familiar spotty face peered over the edge. Yves Galoupe scrambled down the bank. "Is that your bike?" I nodded. "And your name, it is Rosemary Hoyt, that's right?" Another nod.

"Why aren't you in school?" I folded my arms across my chest to hide my embarrassing breasts.

50

"Why aren't you?" he flung back.

"I was sick this morning. I'm better now."

"*Moi aussi*." His smile was mischievous. "Sometimes when I am too sick of Americans, I depart from my school for a while."

"What do you mean sick of Americans? How come you're insulting us? You're a guest in our country."

He turned a dark red. "She says the same." He picked up a handful of rocks, "and says and says and says." He threw rocks into the water so hard that drops jumped out, splashing me.

"Quit it! Are you living with her? My friends said you lived at Lawrenceville School."

He shook his head. "I do. Living with her was too terrible . . ." He rolled his rrs the way my French teacher begged us to do. "She's worse than the Nazis." His face changed, his eyes darkened . "No, that is not true. Nothing is worse than them."

The look in his eyes frightened me, but I couldn't help asking, "What did they do?"

He turned and spoke so low I could barely hear, "My family, we were on the list for a prison camp. When they take you on the train to one of those camps, you never come back."

Prison camp. I didn't want to hear the rest of his story.

Yves picked up another handful of rocks and hurled them across the stream. Then another, then another. Finally, he turned to face me. He looked calmer. "Truthfully," he said, "Kitty is not so bad. She is just, what you Americans call, a real pain in the ass."

I burst out laughing. "You can't say that."

"No?"

"The word ass is rude."

"Kitty says it."

"She's rude . . . oops, sorry."

"That is okay." Yves put his hands in his pockets and looked up at the sky. "Next week, The Lawrenceville School is having a tea dance. Would you like to come with me?"

"M-me?" I was astonished. "Why don't you ask Lucy?"

He drew his dark eyebrows together. "Who?"

"L-lucy, the blonde girl at Mrs. Wainwright's party. She likes you." He still looked puzzled. "You know," I said, growing impatient, "you met her at the party where the dog dragged the turkey on the floor and got it all hairy."

He grinned. "I do not forget the turkey. But I do not remember any girl except you." Then sounding almost timid, "Will you come?"

I started quaking inside. "I-I don't think I can."

"You do not want to go with me?" The corners of his mouth turned down.

"No, it's not that. But I've never been to a dance and . . . well, maybe next year."

He threw some more rocks. "It is only a daytime dance. Even if you are *jeune fille*, I think your mother would let you go."

I thought *jeune fille* sounded a lot better than a little kid. I put up one hand and touched my neatly pinned braids. "And I don't have anything to wear."

Yves said, "Wear the clothes you wore to the turkey party."

I couldn't imagine myself at Lawrenceville with a date. "But I don't know how to dance."

"I am very good dancer," Yves said smugly, "I will teach you."

"Why do you want me to come with you?"

Yves smiled. "Because you are funny and also, I think, you have a good heart."

I felt pleased, but also flustered. "Ask me again and I'll say yes."

"Not this time?" He put his head on one side studying me.

"I don't think my mother . . . hey, I've got to go."

Yves stepped closer. "Maybe I could visit your house one day and show your mother I am not such a bad dragon."

His eyes looked sad. Suddenly I put myself in his place. He was living in a foreign country with no mother and a father who went off to play the piano leaving Yves with a woman he couldn't stand.

"Sure, you can come any time. But I warn you my grandfather is a terrible cook."

"All Americans are terrible cooks." His smile was crooked. "Do you come here often?"

"Only when I'm fed up."

"*Moi aussi.*" We picked up our bikes. "Maybe we will meet here again."

I waved.

On the way home, the green fields looked brighter and the trees had sharper edges. Zooming past the cow, I shouted "Halloo!" at her. I was feeling much better.

Monday, May 4, 1942
Sugar Consumers With A-H Names Line Up Today
Foe Strikes To Within 30 Miles of China

Chapter Eleven

Wading in that freezing brook made me catch me a big cold and a fever. The next time Lucy telephoned, I really *was* too sick to talk to her. Besides, I hadn't quit worrying about how she might worm out of me what I didn't want to say—that the Goodmans had a lot of black market stuff in their house.

I was thinking about it so much that when Teddy stopped by my room, I blurted out, "I think the Goodmans use the black market. I saw a huge pile of candy and nylons and cigarettes at their house. Don't you think it's terrible of people to cheat their own country when we're at war?'

Teddy frowned. "Rosemary, we are not put into this world to judge people."

I sniffled. "That's all right for saints like you, but . . ."

Teddy put up one thin finger. "I am *not* a saint," he said firmly, "I just follow the leading of my inner voice. As thee must learn to listen to thine."

I didn't say anything. How could I confess to my grandfather that I'd never heard a peep from my inner voice? Not even during the one time I went with him to an endless Quaker meeting. I'd squirmed on the hard wooden bench and when the silence went on too long, sang in my head all the Hit Parade songs I knew. But the whole time I was there my inner voice had absolutely nothing to say.

Now Teddy said, "It is my inner voice that tells me I must I speak against the war. I am sorry it troubles thee and also thy mother . . . incidentally, has thee apologized to thy mother for shouting at her?"

I nodded. Mum had accepted my apology, but she didn't stop urging me to make it up with Lucy. If only she knew how hard I was trying.

By the time I went back to school, I'd almost forgotten about the Goodman's black market hoard. But it came back to me when I looked up at the front porch and saw Lucy and Mona hanging over the railing, making frantic arm signals telling me to come up there. I gritted my teeth and drove my fingernails into the palm of my hand. I told myself to be strong.

"Spill the beans, Rosie," cried Lucy, "*toot sweet.*"

Behind me, Kat got out of her limousine and slammed the door.

I turned to her and said, "Hi."

She marched past me without a word.

Lucy giggled. "Oooh, what did you do to her?"

"Nothing," I said truthfully, wondering what made Kat look so stone-faced.

In math class, Kat sat up front. She was good in math and she usually waved her hand around like an eager beaver trying to get the teacher to call on her. Today her hand stayed down and so did her head. What was going on?

After class, I tried to catch her in the hall, but even with her stiff knee, Kat got down the stairs before I could reach her.

At recess, the club members dragged me out to the playground. The Lower School girls were jumping rope and chanting, "Teddy bear, teddy bear, turn around, Teddy bear, teddy bear, touch the ground." How I wished I were still in fourth grade.

"Tell, tell!" The club girls surrounded me.

I took a deep breath. "Their house is enormous." That was safe. "Long silk curtains, a big white piano and oh, they have this thing called a television."

Mona hissed. "Skip the boring stuff. How much money do they have?"

"Kat says her parents don't talk about money."

"That's a lie. Jews always talk about money," Lucy said.

"How would you know? You don't even know any Jews."

Lucy hesitated. "My father told me."

"What makes your father such an expert on Jews?"

"He works with them, stupid."

"What else did you see out there?" Mona demanded.

"A picture of Clark Gable talking to Kat."

"Wow!" someone said.

Lucy narrowed her eyes. "What are you trying to pull, Rosie?"

"What do you mean? I just mentioned Clark Gable because he's your idol. Aren't you impressed that Kat knows him?"

Lucy's nose twitched. "Rosie, you're hiding something. I can always tell. What is it?"

"N-nothing."

Lucy's eyes were bright. "I don't believe you."

I pressed my lips tight and called on my inner voice. As usual, it had nothing to say.

"Now let's see," Mona ticked off her fingers, "We've covered money . . . the piano . . . oh I know, what kind of food did they have?"

Food was a safe subject. Dizzy with relief, I said, "Iced cakes and crab sandwiches."

"Where'd they get the sugar for the cake?" Lucy leaned forward. "I know," she said, "you found out they use the black market!"

I jumped. Too late, I shouted, "No!"

Lucy's eyebrows went up. "That's what you're hiding, isn't it? You found out the Goodmans use the black market."

I backed away from her. "I didn't say that. I didn't! I didn't!"

I spent the rest of the morning avoiding everyone. I ate lunch alone with a book propped up in front of me. The last class of the day was Music. Grade Eight took it with Grade Six and Seven in the music room, a room with huge windows.

Miss Delahaye, our music teacher, was a small woman who wore high necked black dresses and screwed her dark hair into a tight bun.

56

When she conducted music, her arms whirred like a hummingbird and perspiration fogged her black rimmed glasses.

We started our singing session with "Jerusalem". I loved that song. I sang as loud as I could the words about "burning bows and chariots of fire."

When we finished, Miss Delahaye pushed damp strands of hair off her face. "Good. Now do it again. More emphasis on the altos."

Mona raised her hand. Miss Delahaye nodded, and Mona sidled up to her. She whispered in Miss Delahaye's ear. The teacher glanced around, took off her glasses and polished them on a handkerchief. Mona smiled her awful kitty cat smile and tripped back to her seat.

What was going on? I twisted around. Mona whispered something to Lucy. Lucy whispered to the next girl and so on down the row. The room was quiet. Outside, the mowing machines roared and a fresh grass smell drifted in the windows. My armpits felt wet.

"Ah class . . ." Miss Delahaye wet her lips, ". . . ah, I have just been reminded that perhaps 'Jerusalem' is a poor choice for your group to sing."

What?

The teacher spread her small hands. "Mona has informed me one of you might be offended by it because . . ." *Oh Mona, how could you?* ". . . she is not a Christian." Miss Delahaye's voice slowed like a music box running down.

All eyes turned to Kat. She was calmly looking at her music book.
Silence. Finally Miss Delahaye said, "Enid Goodman?"
Kat looked up. "Yes?"
"Does it offend you to sing 'Jerusalem?'"
"No, why should it?"
"I just thought . . ." Miss Delahaye sunk her little teeth into her lower lip.

"Because I'm Jewish?" Kat lifted her thick eyebrows. "Really, I don't give a darn what we sing."

Wow, Kat deserved a medal for coolness under fire!

A girl from Grade Seven raised her hand. "Miss Delahaye, let's sing 'Ave Maria' . . . oops . . . sorry," she squeaked, then stopped and put her hands over her mouth. Her whole row burst into giggles.

Miss Delahaye had a panicky look on her face. I tried but couldn't think of a single song that wasn't religious. The room throbbed with nerves.

Miss Delahaye breathed in fast and tapped her baton. "Open to page 90 in your songbooks. 'Three Little Maids from School'. All together now."

I wished I'd thought of that song. If I'd raised my hand and suggested it, that would have shown Kat I was not a part of Mona's mean trick.

Miss Delahaye kept me after class to give me assignments I missed when I was sick. I didn't see anybody until the end of school when we all went to the front porch.

Lucy and Mona stood together, looking at me and smirking. I went up to them. "That was a dirty trick you played on Kat."

Mona hissed softly, but kept the pussycat smile on her face. "You're entitled to your opinion, Rosemary. Isn't she Lucy?"

Lucy looked really embarrassed.

"Rosemary," Mona sounded fake sweet. "It's O.K. You can tell us all about the black market stuff now."

"I never said . . ."

"Oh yes, you did." Mona raised her voice, "you said you found out the Goodmans used the black market."

"Louse! Bedbug!" Kat Goodman's furious voice hit me like a hammer. "You told David you would be my friend, but you lied."

I ran over to Kat. "*They're* lying. They made that up."

"Ah, who cares?" Kat twisted her hands together. "If you knew what was going on . . . nah, never mind. You wouldn't care. Just stay away from me, that's all I ask." She limped to the other end of the porch and stared down at the driveway.

I rounded on Lucy and Mona. "How am I supposed to make friends with her when you pull nasty stunts like that?"

They looked at each other and giggled.

Monday, May 4, 1942
4 Destroyers Launched In An Hour
Air Raid Reported on Copenhagen

Chapter Twelve

Standing on Albert Einstein's small wooden porch, I fidgeted. I brushed hair out of my sweaty face. It was too quiet. No cars drove down Mercer Street. The only sound besides my thudding heartbeat was two bumblebees buzzing in the purple blossoms of the wisteria vine.

Desperation had driven me to Einstein's door. Since the day I came back to school, Kat had avoided me. When I tried to phone her house, the maid said Miss Kat was not taking any calls. I hadn't said a word about those nylons, Hershey bars and cigarettes, but I felt just as guilty as if I'd blabbed.

Now I tried to get up the nerve to ring Einstein's bell. If he answered, I'd invite him to come to Miss Worth's War Relief Assembly and play his violin. If he came, I'd introduce Kat to him after the program. Then she might start speaking to me. Then I could tell her the truth about what Lucy and Mona said. And then? Who knows.

Right now, standing on his porch, I wasn't even sure what I wanted. Of course, I wanted to get into that club of the popular girls, but Lucy and Mona seemed to be getting meaner and meaner. The problem was if I walked away from them, the only friend I'd have would be Kat. And she wasn't acting very friendly right now. Mum was right. I was a person who did want to have friends. But nice ones, not cruel ones.

I sighed and put my finger on the doorbell and pressed hard. Everybody said Einstein liked young people. When I was tiny and rode my trike past him on the sidewalk, he'd pat my curls and smile. Lucy's sister said one Halloween she and her friends stuck a pin in Einstein's doorbell to keep it ringing. Instead of yelling at them, he came out and played them a song on his violin. They ended up feeling totally ashamed that they'd tried to trick such a nice man.

A girl I knew offered him fudge if he'd do her math homework. Einstein refused, but in the nicest way. Still, it gave me goose bumps to think of asking a favor of a world famous genius.

Nobody answered the bell, so I knocked on the door.

A dark haired woman opened it. "Ja?"

"Albert Einstein, p- please." My courage was leaking out. "I-I'm Rosemary Hoyt and I used to live across the street from Mis … er . . . Professor Einstein," I said. "Not that he really knows me, not to talk to, I mean, but I need to talk to him now. It's very important."

"He iss not at home," the woman said pleasantly.

"Is he at work?"

"Ja." She nodded and closed the door.

I leaned against the porch post. Now I knew how Eeyore felt in *Winnie-the-Pooh* after his birthday balloon popped. Hopeless.

I could go to the corner where Einstein always turned onto Mercer Street and try to talk to him there. But it had taken all my nerve just to ring his doorbell. Interrupting him as he strolled along with his hands behind his back was not going to be possible. I started walking back to school. I'd be early to meet Mum, but I had nowhere else to go. The Einstein Solution had fizzled.

Friday, May 8, 1942
US Navy Sinks 7 Japanese Battleships
Arctic Fights Costs 5 British Ships

Chapter Thirteen

Mum likes to say, "It never rains but it pours." I used to think that was a dumb expression. But that's exactly how I felt right now. I was in trouble with Lucy and Mona. I was also in deep trouble with Kat. On top of all that, Teddy was sick with pneumonia and it was all my fault.

Here's what happened. We were sitting around after a dinner of potato pancakes and salad, when I said I heard the University was having a rally that night to welcome the Navy V-12s to campus. Teddy pushed his chair back.

"It's just a ruse to encourage more boys to enlist," he said, "I must go there and protest."

"Oh Father, no!" Mum frowned and twirled a strand of hair around one finger.

"But I must, Grace. It's nothing but war mongering."

"How can you call it war mongering, when we're at war?" Mum sighed and lit another cigarette. Teddy headed for the door. "All right, all right," Mum said, "if you insist on going, I want Rosemary to go with you."

Horrified, I jumped to my feet. "Me, why?"

"To keep an eye on your grandfather. I have to stay home with Jackie," said Mum.

I shook my head. I didn't want to go. The whole town would be there cheering for the war. Everyone would see me coming to the rally with my unpatriotic grandfather. They'd think I agreed with him. Didn't I have enough troubles? I turned to Teddy. "Are you going to make a speech?"

He gave me one of his gentle smiles. "No, I will only be a silent witness for peace."

But everyone would know why he was there. And anyone who came with him would be labeled as unpatriotic as he was. Which wasn't fair. I was one hundred percent patriotic.

"You can't make me go!" I yelled at Mum. She had a stubborn look on her face. "What if the Lavalles see me with Teddy? You know how they feel about him. They won't want Lucy to be my friend if they see me there with Teddy."

Mum tapped her cigarette over the ashtray and wrinkled her forehead. "Mmmmm," she said softly. "Yes, I see. You have a point. All right then . . ." she turned to Teddy. "Father, there's a threat of rain tonight. And you have that weak chest. Won't you reconsider and stay home?"

Teddy paused in the doorway. "I am led to witness for peace, Grace."

Mum stood up and paced the room, arms crossed across her chest. "Please, for my sake, please be careful."

"Of course I will be careful, Grace." He kissed her gently on the cheek.

I felt bad as I watched him go. Since he'd been sick, he walked like an old man, back bent and shuffling his feet. Watching him leave I felt like something was squeezing my heart. And also like I as being torn in two pieces. Half of me was loving my grandfather and wanting to keep him safe. I took a few steps toward the door. Maybe, I thought, I should go after all. Make sure he didn't get rained on. But Teddy was already in his car revving the engine. And the other half of me was too ashamed to be seen with him.

I helped Mum clean the dinner dishes while Jackie drew pictures. Then I asked, "Teddy's gone, so can I turn on the radio and listen to the Hit Parade?"

"Yes," Mum said and opened her book. Another mystery. She must have read every one in the library.

I turned the radio low and put my head close to it. I tapped my fingers in time with "Who wouldn't love you?" and tried to whistle when the orchestra did. Jackie made a face at me.

Then my favorite song came on. "I Don't Want to Walk Without You."

Mum looked up, tears in her eyes. "Turn that up louder," she said.

Missing Daddy, I thought and gave her a hug.

We sat peacefully in the living room until we heard the first tap tap tap on the slate roof. Mum jumped and looked through the window into the dark night.

"Rain," she whispered, as the taps got louder and faster. "I hope Father had the sense to get in his car before it starts to pour."

Now the minutes dragged slowly. We all kept looking at the clock. Usually driving from the Princeton campus took only fifteen minutes. Teddy had been gone for over an hour. More time passed and still Teddy hadn't come home. The rain was coming down in buckets. I turned the radio off and hunched over in my chair, biting my little fingernail. Mum sent Jackie off to bed. When he whined about it, she shouted, "Jackie" so fiercely that he scurried upstairs.

We sat in silence until Mum whispered, "Oh Father, thee must come home. Thee must. We need thee."

I'd never heard my mother use the Quaker "thee" before.

"He's probably just waiting until the worst of the rain is over," I said as I twisted my hair into a thick rope. "I just saw a flash of lightning. Maybe he's afraid to drive with electricity in the air."

Mum clasped her hands so tight her knuckles turned white.

When we heard Teddy's LaSalle turn into the driveway, we both shot out the front door. The car stopped near the barn. Nobody got out. We ran to the door and found Teddy slumped over the wheel.

"Oh Father," Mum tugged at his arm. "Let me help you. Oh God, you're burning up."

"Fine . . ." he mumbled. "Just . . . a mo . . ." his head went down.

"Get in on the other side of the car, Rosemary. You push and I'll pull. When we get him out, come around and help me get him inside."

Tugging and pulling and dragging Teddy, we somehow got him into the house. Mum and I were soaked to the skin in just those few minutes. Teddy had been wet for much longer. And he was old and he had a weak chest.

We laid him on the sofa. Mum sent me upstairs for blankets while she pulled off Teddy's shoes and his suit. "Bring a lot of towels," she yelled.

Teddy had started to shiver by the time I came down. His teeth chattered as he said, "A l-l-little d-dust up on the c-campus. S-some angry s-students . . ."

"Don't talk," Mum grabbed towels to rub his wet hair. "Put those blankets over him, Rosemary."

He turned to me. "G-Goodman boy came to my r-rescue."

"Please, Father, save your strength. This could be pneumonia. I'm calling the ambulance."

"D-don't f-fuss," Teddy said, but his voice was feeble.

Mum went to the phone and I took over rubbing Teddy's sparse white hair with a towel. My heart felt heavy with guilt. If I'd gone with him, maybe I could have gotten him to come home before it rained.

"G-g-grateful . . . to me because t-they f-found cousins. Not g-good n-news though."

"Shhh," I said, though I was dying to know more about the Goodman cousins.

". . . Believe," Teddy's eyelids were closing, ". . . horrors Hitler is visiting upon J-Jews." A delicate snore.

"The ambulance is coming," Mum said. "I told them to hurry."

Monday, May 11, 1942
Churchill Warns Nazis of Gas Reprisals
US Reveals Army Bombers Raided Tokyo

Chapter Fourteen

Teddy was sick. So sick Mum barely left his hospital room. Except at night.

The third day he was there, she said as she drove us to school, "Rosemary, why don't you walk down to the hospital after school? Maybe your grandfather will be well enough to see you."

Well enough to see me?

In math class, a new girl sat down next to me. "Heard about your grandfather. It's a shame." I nodded, my throat too clogged to speak. "My mother says," the new girl opened her math book, "this town will be sorry to lose him."

Lose him? I swallowed, but still couldn't talk.

The new girl's name was Anne. "Did you hear about the Graduation Dance?" I shook my head, not interested. "The Upper School voted that eighth graders can come this year."

"Rosemary and Anne, please be quiet," said the teacher.

Anne passed me a note. *"You have to bring a date. Who will you ask?"*

I was too worried about Teddy to think about some dance. I kept going over and over how I should have been at that rally. Should have made him go home before he got wet. I chickened out and that made it my fault that he was in the hospital.

At recess I was leaning against the wall, watching fourth graders play Capture the Flag, when Lucy strolled up to me. "Rosie, you've been avoiding me. Something the matter?"

"Oh no, nothing's the matter," I tossed my head. "If you don't count you and Mona lying about me." She gave me a fake surprised look. "You said I told you how Kat's family used the black market." I balled up my fists. "That was a lie and you know it."

Lucy patted her black velvet hair band and looked over my shoulder. In a low voice, she said, "Uh . . . that, uh . . . wasn't my idea." She whispered, "Look, Rosie, sometimes I have to do things I don't exactly enjoy."

When I stared, Lucy turned pink. "You don't know what it's like. Mona pushes me around at school and Mom pushes me around at home." In a high voice, "Be nice to Mona, dear. Her mother's in charge of the dances at the Present Day Club." Lucy stopped. "Besides, Mona's getting me a blind date for the Lawrenceville tea dance."

I couldn't help it. A smile twitched the corners of my mouth. "What happened to that French boy you liked?"

Lucy scratched her ear and looked down. "Mona says I can do better." Then she looked at me suspiciously. "You're not going, are you?"

Another small smile. "That's for me to know and you to find out."

Lucy's nose quivered, a sure sign she was curious. "Want to go to Renwick's after school?"

"Can't." My smile vanished. "Teddy's in the hospital."

"I heard," Lucy said. In her old voice, "I'm sorry, Rosie."

"Yes." I blinked away tears.

We looked at each other for a long time.

Then Kat Goodman limped across the playground toward us, clutching two enormous knitting needles. Kat hadn't said one word to me since the day she called me a bedbug and a louse. Now she walked right up to me and just stood there.

I pointed to four inches of navy blue knitting hanging off Kat's needles. "What's that?"

"A square. You can make a bunch of them, sew them together and they make a blanket for a soldier. Or you can knit scarves for soldiers. Want some wool?"

"Sure." How come all of a sudden she was acting friendly? I cleared my throat and steadied my voice. "Did you hear my grandfather was in the hospital?"

"Yep." Kat didn't say she was sorry.

"He . . . he said your brother helped him at the war rally when some angry students came after him."

"Yeah, people who are against the war aren't very popular these days. Some guys tried to rough him up. David helped him get away. I wouldn't have raised a finger to help him."

I gaped at her. "Why?"

"I won't protect anyone who's not against Hitler."

"He's a Quaker, I told you. Quakers don't believe in fighting wars. Teddy said your brother told him the Quakers had located your cousins."

She bared her teeth. "Did he tell you what Hitler did to them?" She limped away.

"Hey," I yelled at her back, "I didn't say what Lucy and Mona said I did."

She turned, and said in a sad voice, "It doesn't matter, Rosemary. Not any more. Nothing matters except winning this war. If you want wool for knitting, come to the science lab after school."

"I can't. I have to go see my grandfather."

Walking down Nassau Street, five or six people stopped me to ask about Teddy. I was surprised so many people knew he was sick.

At the corner of Nassau and Witherspoon Streets, I spotted a bushy gray head. It was Professor Einstein, strolling along, his hands behind his back, gray smoke from his pipe curling around his head. Did he know about Teddy? If he said anything to me about my grandfather, maybe I'd find the nerve to ask him to come to our school assembly. As he passed, I held my breath, but Einstein never turned his head.

Teddy's hospital room was bare and white and smelled too clean. Teddy lay on the high bed with a transparent tent over his head.

When I walked in, Mum stood up. "Oh good." She pointed to a big tank with tubes that ran under the tent. "I can't smoke here because of the oxygen."

I walked slowly over to Teddy's bed. His eyes were closed. His chin was covered with white stubble that made him look like a stranger. My heart thundered. I wanted to run.

A nurse in a crackling white uniform bustled in. "Professor Cope," she shouted. "Wakie, wakie. We've got a visitor."

I put one hand on her arm. "Never mind. If he's asleep, I can come back later."

"No, he'll want to see you," the nurse unzipped the tent. She leaned over Teddy. "It's your pretty granddaughter, dear. Wakie, wakie." Teddy opened one eye, then the other. His gray gaze moved around the room until it found me.

"Hi," I croaked, "h-how are you?" *Oh God, what a stupid question.*

"He's coming along, coming along," the nurse moved away from the bed. "I'll leave this thing off his face, so you two can chat." At the door, she said softly, "not for long though."

Teddy beckoned and I shuffled closer.

"I should have brought flowers," I tried to hide my guilt with a gush of words, "gosh, what a dope, why didn't I think? There's tons growing at the house—roses and lilacs and violets and down in the field, there's buttercups and . . ."

He raised his hand to stop me. His voice was clear, but he had to stop to catch his breath between words. ". . . Spirit . . . led . . . me. I am . . . content . . ." Long pause. ". . . Even if I don't . . ." he broke into painful sounding coughs.

His sunken eyes frightened me. "Teddy, you're going to get well. You've got to!"

"Thee must . . . let the Spirit lead *thee.*"

How could I admit I didn't know how to start?

Teddy began coughing again. When he got his breath back, he wheezed, "Center down."

Another mysterious Quaker expression.

Teddy paused. "Listen . . ." he struggled to get out the next words, ". . . inner voice . . ." more wheezing.

"Don't talk." I put my warm hand on his cold one. "I'll center down, I promise. And I'll try to listen to my inner voice, I swear I will, and don't worry . . ."

"In . . . silence." His pale eyes twinkled.

Suddenly I remembered a Memorial Parade Teddy took me to the year I turned five. I wheedled him into buying me two cotton candies and a Popsicle. Just as the Princeton High School band went past, I threw up all over my pink linen dress. Teddy calmly carried me over to a fountain and cleaned off my face and hands with his big white handkerchief. Then he led me back to watch the end of the parade.

When people edged away from my horrible smell, Teddy ignored them. He hummed along with the band and tapped his foot. Other people's opinions didn't matter to my grandfather. Now I realized even if I'd gone with him to the war rally, I couldn't have stopped him witnessing for peace. Teddy did what he thought was right.

I wanted to ask him where he got enough courage to defy the whole town. To be the only person who spoke against the war. There were other things I wanted to ask him, but he was too sick. Tears ran down my cheeks and into my mouth.

Teddy patted my hand again. "Listen . . . inner . . . voice."

The nurse with the crackling skirt returned. "Enough talking for today." She zipped Teddy back into his oxygen tent. Teddy lifted one hand in a tiny wave, then closed his eyes.

I rushed into the hall. Blinded by tears, I ran past the elevators and had to retrace my steps.

As I passed the nursing station, I heard two nurses talking.

One said, "The Professor didn't look too good this morning."

"Bad lungs," the other answered. "Doctor Ford couldn't believe he went out in the rain. Said a man that smart ought to know better."

I slipped around the corner to eavesdrop.

The first voice said, "What chance does the doc give him?"

Mumble mumble. I had to strain to hear. "Says it'll be a miracle if he makes it through another day."

Oh. I ran to the staircase door, pushed it open and sat on the steps, letting the tears fall freely.

Chapter Fifteen

That was the last time I saw Teddy. Mum wanted to have his funeral at Trinity Episcopal Church.

Over and over I insisted, "Teddy would want us to have it at the Quaker Meeting House."

"Rosemary, nobody has enough the gas to get there. The Meeting House is way out in the country. Besides," Mum frowned at me through a cloud of cigarette smoke, "sitting in silence makes people nervous."

"Teddy wouldn't care if they got nervous," said Jackie who hadn't drawn any Nazis since Teddy died. "Teddy wouldn't give a hoot."

I gave Jackie a pat on his cowlick, "Two against one," I told Mum with a shaky smile. "Think about it. If nobody comes, we can blame it on gas rationing. But if nobody came to Trinity . . ." I let my voice trail off.

Mum stubbed out her cigarette and lit another. "All right. All right." She dabbed at her tired eyes.

I put an arm around her. "Come on, Mum. Do what Teddy would want."

She sniffled. "But your friends won't be able to come to the Meeting House."

I faked a smile. Lucy and her gang wouldn't come to Teddy's funeral if we held it in the middle of Nassau Street. "My friends hate funerals."

"I don't have any friends," Jackie said. "So don't worry about me."

I patted his cowlick again. Sometimes my little brother seemed almost human.

Only fifteen people came to Teddy's service. I bet Teddy would laugh if he knew the only people representing the University were the President and the janitor who cleaned his office.

The small crowd sat silently on the hard wooden benches of the Meeting House. I passed Kleenex to Mum, pinched Jackie when he wriggled, studied the backs of people's heads and wished somebody would say something.

I tried, I really tried, to center down and listen for the Spirit. All that floated into my mind were images of Teddy gardening in his old gray sweater, Teddy chopping celery for his awful casseroles, and Teddy teaching me to swim in the muddy pond behind the house.

I thought about how he'd never see the latest kittens turn into cats and my throat got thick. But I swallowed and swallowed and managed not to cry. It was peaceful here, almost as if Teddy were sitting beside us.

I heard the back door open and turned. David Goodman in a black suit walked in beside a handsome woman. She wore a black dress and black hat with a dotted veil covering her face. I looked for Kat, but she wasn't there.

Mum turned to stare at the Goodmans then turned back to me frowning. I put my thumb in my mouth and chewed on a hangnail. She pulled it out, hissing, "Stop that!"

When the service finally ended, I hurried outside. "David," I called.

He had turned to leave, but stopped and shook my hand. "He was a good man."

I looked at Mrs. Goodman who was standing a little distance away. She put a handkerchief up to her eyes, but didn't speak.

"Where's Kat?" I asked David.

"Ah . . . she's been kind of busy." His cheeks were red. "Lots of . . . ah . . . things to do."

"She didn't want to come, did she?"

David grabbed his mother's arm. "Talk to her yourself," he called over his shoulder as he led his mother toward the black limousine.

Mum was shaking hands with people. Her gray skirt and jacket looked too big for her. The Navy wouldn't give Daddy leave to come home.

"Were those people related to your Jewish friend?" she asked.

"She's not my Jewish friend," I said, trying not to lose my temper. "She's Kat. Kat Goodman. And yes, that was her mother and her brother David. Teddy helped get their cousins out of Germany. He saved them from Hitler because they're Jews just like the Goodmans." I realized I was shouting.

Mum said, "Shhh, Rosemary." She turned to a sweet faced old couple and said, "My father would have been so pleased that you were able to be here."

The old farmhouse seemed dark and empty. Teddy's gray sweater still hung on a hook in the back hall and every time I passed it I got a lump in my throat. Mum had made macaroni and cheese, but the sauce came out lumpy. Jackie and I looked at our plates, then at each other. We sighed, picked up our forks and tried to eat the gluey mess. When the phone rang, I jumped up to answer.

It was Lucy. "Sorry about your grandfather," she said, sounding cheerful. "My mother says we should try to remember him the way he used to be." Pause. "She also said to tell your mother she was sorry we couldn't come to the funeral. We didn't have enough gas."

Mrs. Lavalle was Mum's oldest friend. Why didn't she call Mum herself?

"My date at Lawrenceville was terrific," Lucy babbled. "Caldwell Jones. A hockey player. From Buffalo. Boy am I glad I didn't get mixed up with that dreary French boy."

Then I got it. Lucy hadn't called to say she was sorry Teddy died. She called to boast about her stupid blind date.

She kept talking. "For the next Lawrenceville dance, I'll ask Caldwell to get you a blind date."

"Thanks." I grinned because by the next dance, I'd decided to go with Yves. I doodled dancing bugs on the phone pad. Suddenly I was feeling better.

Lucy asked, "Did Kat Goodman come to your grandfather's funeral?"

"No." I didn't mention David and Mrs. Goodman. If Lucy made some nasty crack about them, I might blow up.

After a long silence, Lucy said, "She's nagging us about knitting those ugly squares. If you don't take her wool, she calls you unpatriotic. The girl's turned into a fanatic about the war."

"What's so bad about that? When Teddy didn't support the war, you and your mother called him a traitor. Now Kat is supporting the war and you call her a fanatic."

"You know what I mean," Lucy sounded huffy, "She never shuts up about it . . . .yak, yak yak. War war war."

"I bet lots of kids are knitting squares for her."

Lucy coughed again. "Not our group. I've been talking to the club, Rosie. You're going to have to choose between us. Either you're on Kat Goodman's side or ours."

I banged the phone down.

Fuming, I went back to the table. I hadn't planned to hang up on Lucy. But she'd made me so mad. What I'd just done might have ruined my chances of getting into her club. The funny thing was— right now I didn't care.

Wednesday, May 20, 1942
Allied Vessels Sunk By U Boats
Nazis Challenge Big Channel Sweep by RAF

Chapter Sixteen

With Teddy gone, I felt like I was lost in some woods and couldn't find a path that would get me out. Daddy wasn't here to give me advice. Mum seemed too fragile for me to pester her with my questions. After the funeral, I stayed at home as long as I could, telling myself Mum needed me. Apparently she didn't agree. She sent me back to school at the end of the week.

Most of my teachers said nice things about Teddy. Mrs. Hazeltine didn't mention him. She sat in front of our class, looking like a ghost who'd forgotten to put on lipstick. She told us to read the next chapter in *Ivanhoe*. As soon as we picked up our books, she took out a dirty creased letter, opened it and peered at it. Then she sighed, folded it and put it back in the envelope. Probably from her husband.

After home room, we had English, then Math. Kat slouched past me in the hall. She was knitting a long navy blue scarf that practically dragged on the floor.

I pulled her sleeve. "Hey, if you want me to knit, you gotta give me some wool."

She turned, raising her thick eyebrows. After a moment, she lowered them and gave me a blank look.

Words tumbled out of my mouth. "Listen, what those girls said I said, well, I didn't say that. All I said was that your house was fancy and the food was good."

"I don't give a hoot what you said. Or what they said."

"If you're not mad at me, then how come you didn't come to Teddy's funeral?"

"David and Mom went. Wasn't that enough for you?" Almost a sneer.

"I don't get it. You asked Teddy to help. And he did. His Quakers found your mother's . . ."

Kat's needles clattered. She made a choking noise. "I can't forgive anyone who doesn't want to fight Hitler." Louder. "We have to fight Hitler. We have to beat him. He's a monster. We have to grind his face into the dirt."

I smiled. "I thought you weren't going to get emotional about the war."

"Oh shut up." Kat bent over her knitting and picked up a dropped stitch. "If you knew . . ."

My temper snapped. "You keep saying that. If you knew, if you knew. How can I know if nobody tells me?"

Kat narrowed her eyes. "You really wanna know?"

I felt a cold shiver go through me. Did I? Then I lifted my chin. "Sure," I said.

"Okay, come to the science lab at lunch. You can get some wool and we'll talk."

At lunchtime I found Kat sitting on a stool in the lab knitting the long navy scarf. On the floor beside her was a big bag filled with balls of bright wool. She flapped one hand at it. "Take your pick. Red, green, yellow . . . got needles?"

I nodded.

I chose a red ball and a green one. It would probably take me till Christmas to finish a scarf. I was a slow knitter.

I sat on the stool next to her and pulled out my peanut butter and jelly sandwich. Kat sighed. I put my sandwich down.

"Well?" I said.

Another sigh. "Okay, I'll go back a few years," she said. Her voice dragged the way a record sounds when the Victrola needs winding. "Dad and Mom wanted her cousins to leave Germany and come to America. They wrote and promised to find them places to live etcetera. But the cousins refused to leave Germany. Even though things were tough for Jews, they weren't scared. The Nazis won't dare do anything to us, they said. We have a big business and we pay lots of taxes. Besides, our children don't want to change schools. Change schools!" Kat started laughing, a harsh and horrible laugh that twisted her face and made it look ugly.

I felt like leaving the lab right then. Before she said any more. But I'd asked about her cousins and now I had to listen.

Kat's lip trembled. She looked up at the ceiling and talked in a monotone. "All of them stayed in Berlin." She wiped her eyes with her hand and started knitting again.

I put away my sandwich. When Kat didn't continue her story, I felt relieved. I started inching toward the door.

"No, wait," she said, "let me finish. First the soldiers came and took their husbands away. They needed strong men, they said, to build roads for the Fatherland. Then they grabbed their houses. It was not right, they said for Jews to live in better places than hard working Germans. Soon the whole family had to wear yellow stars on their sleeves."

"Why?"

"To show people that they were Jews, of course." Kat sounded impatient. "That yellow star signed Isaac's death warrant. I'm sure of it."

"What do you mean?" I was shaking inside now.

"Isaac was Rifka's boy, only ten years old. He was blond and blue eyed. Didn't look Jewish. He broke his arm playing soccer. The doc put a big cast on it. And then . . . well, all we know is one day Isaac didn't come home. The family never heard. But I think he ran into some Nazi guy who told him to salute and he couldn't because his right arm was in a cast. So pffft," Kat pulled out an imaginary gun and fired. I shuddered. She gave me a grim look. "That's what I think."

"They wouldn't . . . they couldn't . . ." Bile rose in my throat.

76

"Oh yes, they could. There's nothing Nazis can't do to Jews."
Kat's voice was hoarse. "Leni's girls were twins, fifteen years old.
They were hurrying home from a friend's when the air raid siren
whined. They ran for the nearest shelter. The people inside slammed
the door on them yelling, '*Juden Verboten.*' That means No Jews
Allowed. In the morning they found the girls lying three feet from
the door. A wall fell on them."

I put my fist against my mouth. "I can't believe people would be
so cruel!"

"Nobody does. Believe in that kind of cruelty, I mean. Dad's
leaning on the newspapers to print more stories about what's
happening, but they say there's no proof. Last week the New York
Times wrote that Hitler had sent thousands of Jews to the death
camps. 400,000 French, Polish Jews and Russian Jews were sent to
Germany and where'd they put the story? Buried on page nineteen.
Not a big deal. The Nazis killed half a million people, but they were
only Jews."

I was finding it hard to breathe.

Kat turned and looked right into my eyes. "Tell me, Rosemary,
why don't people care what happens to Jews?"

I looked down. Why *didn't* people care? One of my balls of
wool fell to the floor and I dove for it. When I climbed back on my
stool, Kat was staring out the window.

I cleared my throat. "Are the cousins living with you now?"

"Uh unh." She shook her curly head. "They're in a New York
hospital. I went there. Rifka just sits and stares. She won't talk. Leni,
she creeps around the room hugging the wall. If you get near her,
she screams."

"God!"

"They're Mom's age, but they look older than my grandmother.
Mom takes the train to New York to see them. When she gets home,
she goes to bed with a headache." Kat picked up her knitting. "Now
do you get it why I'm so emotional about the war?"

"Yes." My hands hurt from where I was digging my nails into the
palms.

Kat gripped her needles like daggers and made little stabbing
motions. "If Hitler wins this war, American Jews will be rounded up,
tortured and killed. I want people to know that."

"How?"

"Well first we tell the school."

We? I started to shake my head. But then right out of nowhere, came Teddy's voice, "Rosemary, thee has such a flair for drama." *Hey, what made me think of that?*

"Maybe we could do something together at the War Relief Assembly. That's the one everybody will come to. The whole school, all the parents, half the town will be there." Kat tapped her wooden needles against her teeth. "But I need your help. If it's just me, nobody will listen."

I could feel myself trembling. "What makes you think they'll listen to me?"

Kat pulled out her lunch bag. "Getting late. We should eat."

I pulled bits off my sandwich and tried to swallow them. The bread tasted like paper, the peanut butter stuck to the roof of my mouth. After what I'd heard only a selfish rat would worry about her reputation. Okay, so that made me a selfish rat. If I do something with Kat at the War Relief Assembly, if I tell people what's happening to Jews, I'll be the most unpopular girl in Princeton.

Mum had cooked liver for dinner. It smelled foul. I pinched my nose shut and pretended to vomit.

"Now Rosemary, liver is good for you," Mum said, "and also it doesn't take ration points. Make a salad and set the table please." She turned the meat. "I'll fry some bacon."

As the bacon sizzled, Mum said in an over-casual voice, "Helen Lavalle called today." I stiffened. "She says Lucy says you're spending most of your time with that . . . that new girl."

I banged the forks down on the table. *Lucy, you traitor! Who told me to make friends with Kat in the first place.?*

I tore up lettuce leaves and dropped them in the wooden bowl. "Mum, are you against Kat just because she's Jewish?"

Mum took potatoes out of the oven. "She comes from a different background, dear. She's used to a flashier life. I'm not surprised she doesn't fit in at school."

"Kat would fit in fine if anyone gave her half a chance," I snapped. What would Mum say if she knew about Kat's German family? Isaac, only a year old than Jackie, who was shot because he

78

couldn't salute with a broken arm? The teenage twins, crushed by a wall after they were locked out of an air raid shelter because they were Jewish? Mum was tenderhearted. Would these stories make her cry? Or would she say it didn't matter, because those children were what Mrs. Lavalle called NOKD, Not Our Kind Dear? God, I'd go crazy if she said anything like that.

Jackie walked in, sniffing the air. "Please don't tell me we're having to eat yucky liver!"

I imagined Jackie walking down the street with a big white cast on his arm. I imagined some Nazi in shiny boots ordering him to salute. Frantic, I grabbed my little brother by the shoulders and shook him. "Don't you ever draw another Nazi again, ever, ever, ever!"

"Mum, she's hurting me!" he cried.

"Only an ass would . . ."

"Rosemary!" Mum cried. "Language!"

"I didn't do anything to her," Jackie whined.

"I hate both of you!" I cried and burst into tears. I pulled Teddy's old sweater off its hook and ran upstairs hugging it.

Chapter Seventeen

I curled up on my bed and I cried for a while, then I slept. Later Mum knocked softly and brought me some cookies and milk. When she saw me cuddling with Teddy's old sweater, her eyes filled with tears.

"We can't all be strong like Father," she said softly. I didn't answer. She lit a cigarette and looked around for an ashtray. "Rosemary," she said, "I have nothing against your friend personally. It's just that people in this town can be very narrow minded." I still didn't answer. "We have to go along with the crowd."

Mum emptied out a saucer of red rubber bands and dropped her ash in it. She smiled at me. "A package came today. I was going to save it for your birthday, but I think your father . . ."

"For me? From Daddy?" I sat up. "What is it?"

It was about the size of a shoebox, wrapped in brown paper and string. It was heavy. I tore the paper off. Could Daddy have really sent me my absolute heart's desire?

I ripped the paper off and there was a brown Philco radio. I hugged it, then put it on the table and plugged it in.

A man's voice boomed, "Japanese planes have sunk another American ship." I turned the dial. No horrible war news tonight. Finally, I found Benny Goodman playing "Lady Be Good." I hummed along.

Jackie called up the stairs. "Rosemary. Phone. It's a boy."

Yves's voice sounded very French over the wire. "I am sorry about your grandfather."

"Thanks."

"There is another tea dance next week. Could you come?"

"I'll ask."

Mum said, "Oh Rosemary, not so soon after Teddy's death. It wouldn't look right."

I nodded, then went back to the phone and explained.

"Ah, not *comme il faut*," he said, "I understand." There was a long silence. Then he said in a small voice, "Would it be possible that I come to visit you Sunday?" He sounded lonely.

"Of course. Better come early so you don't have to stay for dinner. My mother's not such a hot cook either. In fact she's worse than my grandfather."

"I will come early."

Sunday, Yves bicycled over from Lawrenceville. Everything started out fine. He admired Teddy's old stone house and barn, then whistled as I walked him through the garden.

"It is like France here," he exclaimed, "very beautiful and old. Not hideous and new like . . ." He stopped, but I could guess he was talking about Mrs. Wainwright's newly built Tudor mansion.

He played Chinese checkers with Jackie who positively glowed. I'd already warned my little brother if he said a single thing about Nazis I'd choke him to death. After hearing Kat's stories, I understood better how dangerous it could be if a person was on the list for a prison camp. "Nobody comes back," Yves had said. I still didn't know what happened to his mother and I didn't dare ask.

Yves seemed fascinated by our books. He wandered around reading titles out loud. "*The Silver Fairy Book*, *David Copperfield* and ah, here is a French one, *Marcel Proust*."

Mum said, "Rosemary's the family bookworm."

"Mum, that's awful. You make me sound like I'm some kind of bug."

"A lady bug, a bug in a rug, a baby buggy," Jackie yelled and looked pleased when everyone laughed.

Mum asked Yves, "Is your father on tour?"

"*Oui*," Yves rumpled his hair. "He gives concerts to raise money for the war."

She said, "So when are he and Mrs. Wainwright getting married?"

Yves clenched both his jaw and his fists. Before he could say anything, I jumped up. "Want to see our kittens? They're in the barn."

In the sweet smelling barn, we searched the hay for the kittens. The mother cat lay in a hollowed out circle with her four babies sleeping around her. Yves pretended kittens were something only girls like, but I noticed his face softened when he picked up the tiny tiger.

It was pretty quiet in the barn, so I started chattering to fill the silence. "I'm glad you came, even if my little brother is so gruesome . . . sorry my mother made that faux pas about your father."

Yves put one hand over my mouth. He turned my head toward his face. When I felt his warm mouth on mine, I closed my eyes. His kiss was sweet, but then I felt his hand wandering from my shoulder down to my breasts.

I jumped to my feet. "If we stay out here too long, my mother will come looking for us. She's pretty jittery these days . . ."Yves tried to pull me down beside him, but I kept on with my nervous talking. "I can't wait until I can come to one of the Lawrenceville dances. Lucy and Mona said they were absolutely great."

Yves pulled away, a strange expression on his face. "They are your friends, this Lucy and Mona?"

"N-no, not really." *What did I just say? Lucy had been my friend since third grade. And she was still my friend. Or was she?*

"I would be sorry to think so." He jumped down and brushed hay off his jacket. "They are not nice girls, *pas du tout*."

"What makes you say that?"

"Never mind."

An old loyalty made me admit, "Lucy and I used to be best friends."

"No more, I hope." Yves ran out of the barn. I sat in the hay, wondering what Lucy and Mona had done to Yves. Then I followed him outside.

He was getting on his bicycle. "Goodbye," he called back, "*au revoir*" and pedaled away before I could ask him what he had against Lucy and Mona.

I set the table while Mum made a meat loaf. As she added breadcrumbs to hamburger, she commented, "I guess I shouldn't have mentioned Kitty Wainwright to that boy."

"He hates her."

"Oh dear. Incidentally, Helen Lavalle called while you two were in the barn. She said Lucy went to a Lawrenceville dance with an adorable date."

"I know. She told me. It was a blind date. Some guy from Buffalo."

"That's actually not why Helen called. She wanted to tell me that at first Lucy was rather interested in Yves."

"Unfortunately," I gave her my sunniest smile, "he wasn't interested in her."

"Rosemary, let me finish!" Fiercely Mum squashed the meat loaf into a pan. "Because when Lucy told her mother she liked this boy, Helen Lavalle naturally wanted to check out his background. We used to all know each other in Princeton, but wartime has brought strangers to town. People we don't know much about. Anyhow, Mrs. Lavalle did some calling around and what do you think she discovered?"

I tossed my head, my cheeks hot. "That Yves is actually Jack the Ripper!"

Mum bit her lip. "She discovered Yves' father is Jewish."

I dropped a fork and bent down to pick it up. *Jewish. Of course. That's why they were on the list for a prison camp. That's why they had to run from the Nazis. But what happened to Yves' mother?*

"Did you hear me," Mum said louder, "I said Yves Galoupe is Jewish."

"Who cares? I mean who actually cares if he's Jewish? Except Hitler, I mean." Mum wheeled around, a shocked look on her face.

"Oh I take that back," I said, beginning to cry, "the Lavalles care. They hate Jews almost as much as Hitler does."

"Calm down, Rosemary, please calm down." Mum washed her hands and moved toward me.

I stepped back and away from her until I was pressed against the sink. "No, I won't calm down, Mum. You don't know what's going on over there. You don't know what Hitler is doing to Jews, and . . . ." I was crying too hard to finish. I kept seeing those murdered children lying on the ground.

"You're upset," Mum said. "Let's drop the subject."

"I don't want to drop the subject," I tried to stop crying. "Why won't you listen to me?"

"I am, I'm listening," Mum said and I saw her tremble. The harsh overhead kitchen light showed every line in her pale face.

"Listen, then. Because this is the truth. Lucy and her new best friend, Mona Maull, have been treating me like dirt all year long. You kept telling me to stay in good with them. So I tried. But they played mean tricks on me and made fun of me. Now they're treating Kat Goodman like dirt. Why do you want me to get along with girls like that?"

Mum twisted the dishtowel between her thin hands. "We don't have a choice," she murmured. It hurt my heart to see how sad she looked. "Princeton is not a big place, Rosemary. The Lavalles and the Maulls control everything; they control what committees women get on, who goes to the parties, who is invited to the dances. Without their approval, you'd have no social life. That's why you must overlook the bad things they say or do."

I stared at her. *Omigod, my mother is flat out scared of the Lavalles and the Maulls.* I felt so sorry for her. She was worried sick that Lucy Lavalle and her mother were going to cut us out of their lives. She expected that would scare me as much as it scared her. But it didn't. All of a sudden I knew I was finished being scared. Of anyone in Princeton.

I took a big breath. Part of me felt as light as if I'd just dumped a heavy load off my back. Another part felt like I was standing on the edge of a cliff getting ready to jump into a deep pool of freezing water.

Tuesday, May 26, 1942
Nazis Stiffen, But Russians Gain
Big US Force Arrives In Ireland

Chapter Eighteen

Anne, the new girl, said, "Mrs. Hazeltine's husband was missing in action for two weeks . . . but yesterday they found him floating on a raft in the Pacific!"

"Wonderful!" I beamed.

"That's not all." Anne gripped my arm. "When Mrs. H. got the news, she called up Sowerby and quit. She jumped on a train to San Francisco and now we have a ghastly substitute."

Lucy glided over, "Isn't that something about Mrs. Hazeltine?" she said. "And I hear Yves Galoupe came to your house Sunday." She did her raised eyebrows routine.

Very calmly, I said, "Lucy, I wish your mother would quit passing along her so-called news to my mother."

Instead of getting mad, Lucy turned pink. "It's just that Kitty Wainwright overheard Yves telling his father about you. So Kitty told my mother and she thought it was her duty to tell your mother that Yves was Jewish."

"Tell her thanks," I said frostily, "for minding my business."

Lucy still didn't look angry. "If you're going to the Lawrenceville tea dance with Yves, I can lend you a dress." She checked me out.

"You used to be shaped like a crayon, but now I think you'd fit into my stuff."

My cheeks burned. "Did I say I was going? Did I ask for your hand-me-downs?"

Lucy's smile didn't waver. "My sister, Nancy, is really good at cutting hair. She said she'd give you a keen haircut."

"Who says I . . . ?"

Someone nudged me. "That substitute looks cranky. We'd better get going."

As we sat in class, I tried to figure out why Lucy was being so nice to me. She must want something. But what?

At recess, the school held its monthly sale of war stamps and bonds. Two seniors sat at a table in the school's front hall, as a line of girls snaked around the white columns. I fingered the dollar bill I'd saved from my allowance. Kat was four girls ahead of me. She turned and waved. In her hand were three twenty dollar bills. Uh oh.

She'd stick out like a sore thumb spending that kind of money. I could almost hear Lucy telling the world how "Jews like to throw their money around."

I pointed to Kat's hand and shook my head. She just grinned. Lucy and Mona were standing right behind her. Once Kat put her money on the table, they'd start a whispering campaign about how she was just showing off that she was rich. I had to do something to distract them.

I skidded out of line and up to the table. I knelt down, and belted out, "Any bonds today?" in a nasal Bugs Bunny voice. People laughed. I moved on to "Praise the Lord and Pass the Ammunition", leaping into the air on the last word.

Someone clapped. I pulled a lock of hair over one eye and tried to imitate movie star Veronica Lake selling kisses to guys who bought war bonds. I was running out of breath, but Kat was almost at the table. Just a few more minutes and I could quit. With my last ounce of energy, I clasped my hands in front of me and sang the first line of "The White Cliffs of Dover".

"Rosemary Hoyt," Miss Sowerby clumped right up to me. "Why on earth are you making such a racket? Please come to my office at once."

I cast a frantic look at the table. Kat was just putting down her money, but everyone else was looking at me. *Whew.*

In the principal's office, I sat on a hard chair, my toes curled, waiting for a lecture on unladylike behavior. It was one of Sowerby's favorite subjects.

"I have a message for you," she said, adjusting her rimless glasses. "Mrs. Hazeltine wanted me to remind you to recite your Shakespeare speech for the War Relief Assembly. I've put you third on the program. Are you prepared?"

I swallowed. "I'm working on it, Miss Sowerby." I wasn't, but it would only take me a day to memorize it. "Isn't it great about Mrs. Hazeltine's husband?"

Miss Sowerby shook her narrow head. "With her gone, I'm short one teacher. This war makes my job extremely difficult. And speaking of which, how is that . . . er . . . new girl fitting in?"

I wondered if I should tell her about Kat's troubles. No, I decided, Sowerby's meddling wouldn't help. "She's fitting in fine," I said, flashing her my Shirley Temple smile.

"That's grand." She pretended to smile back. "It was a bold experiment taking in a . . . uh . . . girl like that, something we might not risk in peacetime. Still, since only one girl of that . . . er . . . persuasion applied, we felt it was our patriotic duty."

I got up and bolted out of the office before I started yelling at her. Our headmistress was a horrible old hag. Couldn't she tell that Kat was a human being, not a "bold experiment?"

Kat was in the science lab at lunch, knitting as usual. When she saw me, she put down her purple square and leaned forward. "What made you stage that one woman USO show?" she demanded.

"You." I pulled out my green and red wool and started to cast on stitches.

"Me?" She wrinkled her forehead. "I don't get it."

"You were waving sixty whole dollars around. In Princeton we don't . . ."

"Don't what? Buy war stamps? Oh come on, Rosemary. Tell me another one."

"Look, five dollars is about our limit. Nobody else had sixty dollars to spend. Buying three bonds would make everyone think you were showing off."

Kat curled her lip, "Holy Cow, what a bunch of idiots. This whole town is crazy . . . except for Albert Einstein of course."

"We're not idiots, we just have our own way of doing things." I said stiffly. *Oh God, I sound just like Mum.* I put a hand over my mouth and giggled.

"What's so funny?" Kat said.

"N-nothing."

"Are you trying to tell me *you* weren't showing off?" Kat said.

"Okay, you're right. I was. I love to perform."

"I can't act," Kat said, staring at her knitting. "But if we band together, we could . . . well, what could we do?"

"I don't know." I twisted my hair into a rope like I always do when I'm nervous.

"We need to tell the school about Leni and Rifka." Kat said. "And we should do it at the War Relief Assembly. Everybody will be there."

"I . . . I'll think about it," I said reluctantly.

Kat opened her lunch bag and bit into her sandwich. After she chewed, she said, "Of course it won't make us any friends. My dad says people want to kill the messenger who brings bad news."

"I know," I said soberly.

I opened my lunch bag. My cottage cheese and olive sandwich didn't look tempting. I fished out one of Mum's rocklike cookies and nibbled on it.

"If you're really going to help," Kat's face was flushed, "we'll have to start right away. We can work at my house, if you want."

Mum would be angry if I went back to the Goodmans. She'd be even angrier if she found out I planned to get up on a stage with Kat. "I just remembered," I said trying to force a piece of the hard cookie down my throat. "Sowerby told me I have to do my Shakespeare speech at the Assembly."

"No weaseling out." Kat grinned. The sun from the window shone through her curly hair, making it look like a brown halo.

The dry cookie stuck in my throat. Just like I was stuck between Mum and Kat. Either I did what my mother wanted or I did what Kat wanted. Whichever way I went, somebody was going to get hurt.

Kat swung her legs. "Did I tell you David's enlisting when school's out?"

"No!" I yelped. The cookie piece shot out of my mouth.

"Yep. Mom's been begging him to stay in school. But he keeps saying evil will triumph if men of good will do nothing. Some famous guy said that, according to David." Kat leaned forward and patted me on the shoulder. "You're a girl of good will, Rosemary."

She's right, I am a girl of good will. But does that mean I have to make the whole school angry at me?

Tuesday, May 26, 1942
Industry In Drive To Get War Scrap
Nazis Hurl Wave of Tanks in Battle Below Kharkov

Chapter Nineteen

For the second time, I pictured myself standing on Einstein's porch. I hadn't planned to return, but I was desperate. Kat would be incredibly mad at me if I didn't team up with her and do something for the War Relief Assembly. But when we told the school what Hitler was doing to Jews in Germany, the school would be horrified. Would they clap or would they boo? Would they be nicer to Kat or would they be meaner than ever? And poor Mum. When she found out what I was doing, her sad face would get some new lines.

When the last school bell rang, I sped out of school, across Stockton and down Mercer until I was half a block away from Einstein's small wooden house.

As I ran, I rehearsed what I was going to say. "Sir, everyone will listen to you, if you tell them how bad things are for the Jews in Germany."

Kat's father told her Einstein had sponsored hundreds of Jewish people who wanted to get out of Europe. He'd sponsored so many refugees the U.S. government wouldn't let him sponsor any more. So he knew about the Jewish situation and he cared. If he told the truth about what Hitler was doing, everyone would listen to him. They always did. And after they listened, they'd applaud.

A black limousine passed me going at a very slow speed. It was even bigger and shinier than the Goodman's. The limousine swung around and parked in front of Einstein's house. Two smaller black cars pulled in to the curb parked behind it.

Men in dark suits wearing city hats jumped out of the smaller cars and surrounded the limo. A chauffeur held the door open and a tall man got out and walked up the path. He stepped into the house and two men in hats followed him in. The other men stood outside, peering up and down the street. Bodyguards, I thought. Wow. The man in the limousine must be really important.

I couldn't go up on Einstein's porch now. With those men staring at me, I didn't even dare walk past his house. I crossed the street and started back to school.

I'd heard how presidents and senators and generals came to Princeton to ask Einstein's advice. Now I knew it was true. Einstein was a really important man. I couldn't bother him with my small problems. Not today. Not any day.

Deep down, something inside me knew all along that asking Einstein for help was a dumb idea. Now I tried to think what plan Teddy would suggest for me. Not to go running to Einstein, that was sure. He'd tell me . . . well, he'd tell me to listen to that little voice inside of me and follow whatever it told me to do. Truthfully, I had no inner voice. But I guessed I already knew what I had to do.

Saturday, May 30, 1942
Nazis Seize Scores In Occupied France
US Air Chiefs Plan Blow At Germany

Chapter Twenty

All the way home and all through dinner, my mind was a jumble of questions. What kind of thing could I do that would show our school what was happening to Jews in Germany? I believed Kat when she said she couldn't act. You have to make a fool of yourself to be a good actor, and Kat wasn't the fool type. With her stiff leg, she couldn't dance. Her singing sounded like someone chain sawing a tree. She could do chemistry experiments, but chemistry had nothing to do with the situation in Germany.

I flopped onto my bed and turned on my radio desperate for an idea. Soap operas . . . no. News . . . maybe. Kat could read the lines like the guys who give war reports every night. But if she were just reading a bunch of lines, what could I do? I turned the dial again.

"Ma'am, what do you think of rationing?" said a male voice. I'd heard this program before. Some man went up and down the New York streets holding a microphone. He'd stop people and ask them questions. Then he'd stick the mike in their face and broadcast their answers.

A woman's voice answered. "I got a hard job filling up my boys—two thirteen year olds and boy do they eat like there's no tomorrow. But I don't mind cutting down on meat, if it helps our boys overseas."

Hey, what if Kat and I did our own *Man on the Street* program? Pretending it was happening in today's Berlin. She'd be the interviewer holding the mike and I . . . I . . . I sat up so I could think better. I couldn't play those dead children. Too sad. But I could maybe pretend to be Kat's mother's cousins. First one, then the other.

"I am Leni," I began trying to imitate a German accent. "And I live in a big house in . . ."

I telephoned Kat. "I have an idea. You know that *Man on the Street* program on the radio? Well, what if you were the interviewer asking questions and I was the cousins? What do you think?"

"Wow, Rosemary. You're going to stand up in front of the school and pretend to be Leni and Rifka? Would you really do that?"

"It's the only thing I can think of."

Kat sounded nervous. "Would they listen to us?"

"I don't know," I said, "but maybe if people hear those terrible stories, it will make them think."

"Maybe," Kat said, but she sounded worried.

"If we're going to do this, I need more information. Like where the cousins lived, what they did, what they wore . . ."

"Oh yeah, yeah yeah. Mom knows all that. She has oodles of clothes too. She'll loan you anything you need." Kat said, sounding like she was warming up to my idea. "And I'll dig the facts out of her. Talking about Leni and Rifka will make her cry, but what's the diff, she cries all the time. Ever since David . . ."

"Is he still planning to enlist?"

"In June." Pause. "Rosemary, think we can pull this off?"

"Sure," I said, trying to sound confident.

Saturday, I went out to Teddy's Victory Garden to pick some carrots. Nobody had worked here since Teddy died and the carrot tops were hidden among the tall weeds. I reached for one and pulled. It didn't come out. Then I tugged on the top so hard that when the carrot finally popped out of the ground, I fell over backwards. "Awk!" I yelled.

"Ha ha that is verry funny." I looked up into Yves' laughing face. "Is it okay that I come on my bicycle to see you?"

"Sure." This was the first time Yves had been here since Mum found out he was Jewish. Praying my mother would act okay, I scrambled to my feet and brushed off my skirt. "Want to go for a walk?"

"Uh huh." He pulled out a crumpled pack of cigarettes.

"My friend told me smoking raises your blood pressure," I said frowning.

"Everybody smokes in France." He raised one eyebrow, then put a cigarette in his mouth and lit it.

We walked behind the barn and down toward the pond where Teddy taught me to swim. The silence went on and on. I had a question for Yves. I took a deep breath, but just the same my voice came out squeaky.

"Uh . . . Class Eight gets to go to the Upper School Graduation Dance. Want to come?"

Yves smiled. "You are allowed suddenly to go to dances?"

"It's weeks away. In June. Mum can't make me stay home forever."

"Then I will come," Yves said. He took a puff, exhaled, then said. "Will your friends be there, that Lucy and Mona?"

"I don't know. Yves, what did they do to you?"

He took another drag of his cigarette. "At the school dance, Lucy comes up to me and says she is forcing you to make friends with a Jewish girl. She laughs like it is a big joke."

"Well, she did force me, and I did make friends with the Jewish girl. Her name is Kat Goodman."

"I am Jewish, you know." Throwing his cigarette down and stamping on it. "Through my father only. Jews say Jewishness arrives through the mother, but the Nazis, they don't care about that. They hunt you down if you have even one drop of Jewish blood in your veins."

"So if your mother wasn't Jewish . . ." I stopped, then rushed on, "but she didn't come to America with you?"

He winced, then looked up at the sky. "It is hard for me to say."

"Then don't. I'm sorry . . ."

"No, I want to tell you this. We are on the run for a month. My father, my mother and me. And then my mother, she got sick. Like in the chest, you know. Coughing all the time. But we couldn't stop. It was too dangerous. Days we walked. At night, we slept in the fields or maybe in cold barns. Often we were wet from rain. *Maman*, she got sicker. And then . . . and then . . ." his voice clogged up and stopped. He turned his back to me.

"I'm so sorry," I said. He nodded.

He just stood there a while. Then he wheeled around, his face not showing any emotion. I wanted to give him a big hug, but I knew he'd be embarrassed, so I tried to keep my face blank too. We walked around the edge of the pond. Yves threw some stones in. Neither of us said anything for a long time.

Finally I broke the silence. "Kat Goodman has relatives who had a terrible time in Germany. She says Americans need to know what's going on."

"They do," Yves said in a choked voice.

"So Kat and I are going to do a sort of skit for the War Relief Assembly."

He looked interested. "How will you do it?"

"It's going to be a radio interview. Kat asks the questions and I will be dressed up like an old woman . . . well, actually two old women and they're not old, but they look old . . . because of what happened to them . . . and their children."

"If you're bring bad news your school won't like it. Or you." Yves sounded weary. "Americans don't want to hear about horrors of the war. They like flag waving and songs."

"I know," I said, "but Kat thinks people have to know what Hitler is doing."

"I'd like to meet this Kat. Will she be at the dance?"

"I-I don't think so."

He scowled. "Because of what those girls say?"

"No. Because she's tall and shy, and has curlier hair even than me and she limps because she had polio."

Yves threw back his head laughing. "*Quel defi!*"

"What's that mean?"

"Ah . . . it is . . . it means I think . . . challenge." He pronounced it *shallawnge*. "So I will have to find her some boy who likes tall limping girls with big hair."

"Hey, she's not that bad."

"I only repeat what you say."

"She has a great figure and she's from California and her father's a movie producer."

"Much better."

"And she needs to take time off from worrying and knitting ugly squares for soldiers."

Yves smiled, put a finger under my chin and pulled me close. The kiss was sweet, but when he tried to put his tongue in my mouth, I pulled back. "Let's go get a Coke."

He raised one eyebrow and smiled at me.

Mum was reading in the living room. I opened two sodas and put some cookies on a plate.

Yves walked over to Mum and put out his hand. "How do you do, Mrs. Hoyt. I hope it is all right that I pay you a visit?"

Mum looked confused. "Of course," she said. Then, "Is Rosemary being a good hostess?"

"*Bien sur*. I mean, yes. She even tells me about this skit she is doing with her friend Kat to tell everyone what happens to the Jews in Germany." I put a hand over my mouth to stifle my gasp. I'd forgotten to warn Yves not to mention the skit in front of my mother. Now there was going to be trouble.

Chapter Twenty-One

Mum didn't say anything about the skit while Yves was there. But as soon as he'd gone, she came after me.

"What's all this about a skit, Rosemary?"

It was a direct question so I had to answer.

She crossed her hands in front of her chest as if she was protecting herself. "Rosemary, Rosemary, you are going to get yourself in such hot water if you do this."

"Who cares?" I shot back. "Did you know Yves' mother died running from the Nazis. She wasn't even Jewish, but the Nazis didn't care. They were going to send the whole family to a prison camp. She got sick and they couldn't stop running, so she died. That's what I call getting in hot water."

"That's awful, of course . . . his mother dying. Oh that poor boy," Mum lit one of her never-ending cigarettes, "but that happened in occupied France. We live in America and thank God there are no Nazis here. For people like us, it's still important to fit in with the crowd."

97

My fraying temper snapped. "Mum, I can't believe you think pleasing Lucy Lavalle and her parents is more important than people dying because they were married to a Jew!"

Dark red patches stood out on Mum's pale cheeks. "But if you team up with this . . . this outsider, and force your schoolmates to listen to these horror stories, you'll make them feel guilty."

"I *want* them to feel guilty!"

Mum put down her book and looked into my eyes. "Rosemary, for your own good, I can't let you do this."

"You can't stop me." Mum's eyes went wide and her mouth fell open. I squared my shoulders and lifted my chin. "I don't care what you say. I'm going to do this skit with Kat."

Mum put a hand over her mouth and she blinked and blinked as if she couldn't believe what I'd just said. I was shaking inside. I'd never defied my mother like this. Never.

With Mum staring at me, I went on, "I promised Kat and I'm not breaking my promise. I'm sorry, Mum. But this is really important."

"Calm down, Rosemary." She wrung her hands. "You're getting over excited."

"I am not over excited. I am standing up for what I believe. That's what Teddy told me to do."

"Don't quote my father to me!" A muscle jumped in Mum's jaw.

"He was a good man," I said, my chin wobbling. *Don't cry, Rosemary. Don't cry.*

"Oh Rosemary, of course he was," Mum touched my shoulder carefully as if she were afraid of setting me off again. "But he was old. His life was finished. You are young and your life is just beginning. I want you to have a good life. I want you to have lots of friends . . ."

"Like Lucy who's only nice to me when she wants something? Or your friend, Mrs. Lavalle, who didn't even bother to call you when Teddy died? Didn't come to his funeral? Great friends they are!"

Mum slumped into a chair, her face pinched.

"Hey, don't look so sad," I said. "Maybe after the war, we'll move out of this lousy town and find a better one where better people live."

"Language," Mum said faintly. She took a deep breath, "I love you, Rosemary, and I want the best for you. You know that, don't you?"

"Yes. And I love you too. But I'm still doing the skit."

Mum searched my face. "How did this Jewish girl manage to twist you around her little finger?"

"She didn't and her name's Kat, Mum. Please stop calling her 'the Jewish girl!'"

Mum got pink. "It's just that before the war, we didn't know any . . . people like that. You hear jokes, of course, but I can't . . . I mean I truly believe they're different."

"How do you know? You haven't even met the Goodmans. Neither have the Lavalles but that doesn't stop them from spreading dirt about them. And girls at school listen to that dirt and pass it on and nobody gives Kat a chance."

"See?" Mum got up. "If you team up with her, you'll be an outsider and nobody will give you a chance. That's what I was trying to tell you." She sighed, "I'm afraid Father was a bad influence on you."

"He was a good influence," I insisted, my hands tightly clenched, "He told me to follow my instincts. He told me to stick up for what was right. And that's exactly what I'm doing."

A faint smile flickered over Mum's face, "You seem to have gotten the backbone that Father tried to instill in me. He'd be so pleased," she said softly. Then more serious, "But Rosemary, a Quaker conscience is not an easy thing to live with."

"Maybe not, but I've got to do that skit."

"Well," Mum gave me a timid little hug, "I don't approve, you know that. But it looks as if nothing's going to stop you. I only hope it doesn't blow up in your face."

"Me too." I hugged Mum back. At this moment, I felt brave and determined. Would I feel the same on the day of the assembly?

Monday, June 1, 1942
Vineland, NJ Empties Its Pockets for $560,000 in War Bonds
1,000 British Bombers Set Cologne On Fire

Chapter Twenty-Two

"Rosemary," Lucy pulled me aside between classes, "my sister says she could make your hair look quite adorable."

"Why is your sister so interested in my hair?"

"Well," Lucy sunk her white teeth into her red lip. "I thought it might be fun if we double dated for the graduation dance."

"Who are you taking?"

She blushed. "Well, nobody yet . . ."

"Lucy Lavalle," I stopped in the middle of the hall, putting my hands on my hips, "are you asking me to get you a blind date?"

She nodded, her face red. "I heard you were going with Yves . . ."

"I am."

"So," she tossed her blonde hair, "you can ask him to fix me up."

"But Yves is Jewish. And you don't like Jews."

She flushed even redder. "He doesn't have to fix me up with a Jewish boy." I stared at her.

Lucy lowered her eyes. "H-hey, R-rosie, if it's the club thing bothering you, I'll take care of it. This afternoon. I swear to God and cross my heart. Come to my house at four and we'll take you in. No kidding."

Once I'd have killed to hear those words. Now they meant nothing.

"Can't make it. Kat Goodman and I practice our skit every day after school."

Lucy's eyes shot sparks. "Do you expect me to believe that?"

"I don't care what you believe. It's the truth."

"Rosie, how can you do this to me? You're my oldest friend."

"Gotta go."

When I looked back, Lucy was still standing there with her mouth hanging open.

I was sitting in a toilet stall a few minutes later when the bathroom door banged open.

"Lucy's got her nerve," Mona stormed. "Asking Rosemary to join our club before the rest of us even got a chance to vote on it."

"She's desperate. Can't get a date for the dance, blind or otherwise." That was Adelaide, another club member.

"Yesss," Mona hissed. "Bill refused to fix her up. Her last blind date said she was a drip." *Mirror mirror on the wall, who's the meanest girl of all? Pee Wee Maull, Pee Wee Maull.*

Adelaide said, "Back to Rosemary, my mother told me the whole point of a club is keeping people out."

"Yeah, I used to love watching Rosemary run around like a windup mouse doing everything we told her to. Lucy felt sorry for her. She said we ought to let her in. But I said no way. I liked watching her try to please us . . . but listen," slowly now, "lately she hasn't been trying so hard. I wonder why."

"Because she's been hanging out with the Jew, that's why." The door banged and they were gone.

I got up and walked to the sink, splashing cold water on my hot face.

So Lucy had invited me into her club just so she could get a blind date. And all this time, Mona and some others had been laughing at me and my pathetic efforts to join their club. I knew Mona was mean, but I'd never guessed just how mean.

I thought some more about that club. Lucy and Mona were both supposed to be in charge, but Lucy was scared of Mona and Mona was so nasty if she bit you, you'd need a rabies test. The rest of the club girls were just "going along with the crowd" as Mum would say. If you gave me a million dollars, I wouldn't join that club now.

I changed into my gym tunic and ran out on the baseball field. I was a terrible baseball player, but when Mona hit a pop fly, I put up my glove and actually caught it. Then I threw the ball to third and made the runner out. When somebody cheered, I punched my hand in my glove and grinned.

After the game, Lucy came up to me. "Rosemary," she gave me her best chipped-tooth smile, "I'll give you one more chance. Come over to my house after you practice and we'll initiate you into the club."

"No thanks." I looked right into her eyes, "Lucy, remember when you called me on the night of my grandfather's funeral and said I had to choose between Kat and your club. Well, I have. I choose Kat."

Lucy gasped, "But we're your oldest friends."

I could hear a sneer in my voice when I said, "Like my old friend Mona Maull, the meanest girl in town? And she's not just mean to me either. Ask her what she said about you."

Lucy's smile disappeared. She ran over to Mona. "Rosie says you've been talking behind my back."

"You believe *her*?" Mona sniffed. "That girl lies like a rug. What do you expect of someone who has a traitor for a grandfather?"

Tears sprang to my eyes. I muttered, "Don't let them get to you," until my voice stopped shaking.

Then I said loud and clear, "My grandfather was *not* a traitor. He did what he thought was right and he didn't care what other people thought." I looked around at all of the club girls. Some looked defiant, some ashamed. "When Kat Goodman came to Miss Worth's, nobody gave her a chance. They heard their parents say bad stuff about Jews and they copied them without even trying to get to know Kat. You've missed a lot. Especially you, Lucy."

Lucy's head jerked up. "So what?"

"So Kat knows Clark Gable. If you'd been nice to her, you could have had his autograph."

Lucy tossed her head. "I don't care."

"Okay, but do you really want to spend the rest of your life being bossed around by Pee Wee Maull?"

Mona hissed and narrowed her eyes. "Stop calling me Pee Wee or you'll never get in our club."

"Why don't you ask me if I want to join your stupid club?" I tossed my head. "My answer is no thanks. And I bet some other girls you boss around would like a chance to make their own friends without asking your permission." Several girls nodded.

Lucy put her hands on her hips. "I'm going to tell my mother what you said. And she'll call your mother and then you'll be sorry!"

"Hey Luce, that's really pathetic."

Watching Lucy hurry over to her so-called friends, I felt like crying. Lucy had been my best friend for so long and now she wasn't a friend at all. Teddy said growth means change and change is always painful. My grandfather was a very wise man.

Wednesday, June 3, 1942
Nazis Raid Canterbury
Churchill Here for Talks

Chapter Twenty-Three

Kat and I rehearsed the skit I'd written every lunch hour in the science lab. At first I felt self-conscious with Miss Stockbridge sitting in the corner. But she never looked up from her book, so finally I managed to throw myself totally into the part—clutching my dress and falling to my knees when I heard about the death of my children.

Kat stared as I pulled my hair and beat my chest. "I'd rather die than make such a fool of myself."

"Thanks a lot, pal." I struggled to my feet. I hoped Kat never found out how much I'd begun to feel like Rifka. Sometimes after we'd practiced, it was hard for me to come back to the real world.

"Sorry." Kat put her bad leg up on a stool. "But the way you scream . . . it gives me chills."

"I'll take that as a compliment."

"I'm worried about asking Mom to come to the assembly. She might have hysterics."

"Is she still worried about David joining up?"

Kat sighed. "She's worried about everything—the war, her cousins, and David. She cried for two weeks straight when we had to have our dog put to sleep. It's like the war pulled some plug inside her and now she can't shut the tears off."

"My mother hates the war too. She's also very nervous about me doing this skit."

The door opened and Anne, the new girl who'd asked me about the Graduation Dance, walked into the lab.

"Who's that?" Kat said, turning to look at her.

"Just me." Anne smoothed her red hair behind her ears. "Uh . . ." she said, "uh, I was wondering what you're doing in here every day."

"Nothing," Kat said firmly. The room was silent.

Finally I said, "Anne, did you ever find a date for the dance?"

"Sure did." When Anne smiled, her braces sparkled. "I asked one of the V-12s. My dad's the commander, so I knew any one of the guys I asked would have to say yes. How about you?"

"I'm going with this French boy and Kat, she's . . ."

"Not going at all." Kat snapped her mouth shut so hard it made her teeth click. "Now if you don't mind . . . er . . ."

"Anne."

"We've got work to do."

"You're doing a skit, aren't you?" Anne said. "Any chance I could be in it?"

I turned to Kat, "What if she played Leni? It's really hard playing both sisters."

Kat didn't answer.

"I like to act," Anne said. "My dad's in the Navy so we move a lot. I make friends by getting into school plays, wherever we go." She preened a little, "I'm good."

"What do you think?" I said. Kat looked at the wall and whistled through her teeth.

Anne took a deep breath. "Here's Beth in *Little Women*," she said. She folded her hands across her stomach and hunched her shoulders, making herself seem shorter and more fragile. Softly, "I'm not like the rest of you, I never made any plans about what I'd do when I grew up, I never thought of being married as you all did. I couldn't seem to imagine myself anything but stupid little Beth trotting about at home. I'm not afraid of dying, but," Anne finished in a voice we could barely hear, "I'll be homesick for you even in heaven."

I had to swallow a huge lump in my throat.

Kat said gruffly, "Yep, you can act all right. But I should warn you being in this skit won't make you popular with the rest of the school. The opposite in fact."

Anne grinned. "So what?"

We waited. Finally Kat nodded.

I turned to Anne. "Leni's the rich sister who gets tortured by the Nazis, I'll copy out your lines, unless you want to make up your own."

"Unh uh," said Anne, "I'll go with yours."

She was word perfect in three days. She could even cry real tears. I hoped Leni's story didn't haunt her as much as it was haunting me.

When we weren't rehearsing I tried to think about happy things. Like the graduation dance.

"Kat," I said, "remember Yves the French boy whose father is a famous pianist?"

"How could I forget? You yak about him all the time."

"I told him to get you a date for the graduation dance."

Kat stiffened. "What did you say?" she said in a frosty voice.

"You heard me. We are going to double date at the dance. I've made up my mind."

Kat stood up. "I'm not going. I don't dance." A quick glance at her leg.

I swallowed. "Did I tell you Yves escaped from the Nazis because they were going to send his family to a prison camp? I think you'll like him. Anyway, he's getting you a date. You're coming. That's final."

"Who says?" Kat folded her arms and pushed out her chin.

"Me. If you don't, I'll quit this skit." My chin went out too.

"You can't . . ." Her eyes flicked over my face. "You're kidding, right?"

I said, "Hey, you can wear that terrific pink and white taffeta dress I saw in your closet. And we'll both sit out the fast numbers. I can't jitterbug and in fact I'm not much of a dancer at all." Kat shook her head. I twisted my hair into a rope and played my last card, "Kat, you've got to come. I need to have a friend with me. I've never been to a dance. I'm scared." This last statement was true.

"Really?" Kat looked doubtful, then peered into her lunch bag and mumbled, "guess I gotta start somewhere." She polished an apple on her napkin. "But if I go to the dance, you gotta do something for me."

"What?"

"Didn't you say you used to live across the street from Einstein?"

"I did."

"I want to meet him."

"Okay," I said, "I'll introduce you. After the skit."

Wednesday, June 10, 1942
US-British Fliers Cripple Italian Navy
War Outlay Nears A Billion A Week

Chapter Twenty-Four

Kat pinched the dusty maroon curtain together with one hand. She made a small peephole with the other. "It's filling up," she announced.

"I feel sick," Anne whispered. She grabbed her wide black hat, which made her armful of rhinestone bracelets sparkle under the spotlight.

"I feel sick too," I said.

The day of the War Relief Assembly had finally arrived. We three were actually going to stand up in front of the whole school and our parents and friends and tell people a whole bunch of terrible stuff they absolutely didn't want to hear.

"You're not sick," Kat said briskly, "you're just nervous."

"O-of c-course we are," my teeth chattered, "aren't you?"

"Why would I be nervous? Hey, there's David!"

I covered my mouth with one hand, terrified I might actually throw up.

Kat peered out again. "Mom's with him. Oh God, I hope she doesn't start bawling."

I wondered if my mother was out there. Were Lucy's mother and Mona's mother in the audience? My stomach churned.

Anne moaned, "Ooooh, I have to pee."

"No time, dimwit," Kat said impatiently, "be like me. I'm fine." She shoved up her raincoat sleeve and showed us her steady hands. "I'm cool as a cucumber."

Miss Sowerby bustled up, "Girls, get away from that curtain. Take your places. The Lower School is ready to go on."

I pushed Kat aside so I could peek out. In the front row Lucy, Mona, and the rest of the club sprawled in their seats, whispering. Bursts of laughter rippled up and down the line. I realized that even if we acted our very best, we wouldn't impress these girls. It seemed like years ago, I'd wanted to join their stupid club.

"Rosemary," Miss Sowerby's stern voice came from behind and made me jump. "Why are you wearing that peculiar black dress? I should think tights would be more appropriate for reciting a speech from Shakespeare."

Tights? Omigod! Sowerby still thinks I'm doing the Henry the Fifth thing. Then it flashed into my mind that we had no permission to do our skit. We'd never asked her if we could do it. Guess I knew she'd say no.

A line of third and fourth graders filed between me and the headmistress. They were headed for the stage. The children kept Sowerby from asking me any more questions, but now my worries boiled up like a spouting volcano.

Kat must have seen me shaking. She pushed me farther back into the wings, "Buck up, Rosemary. It's too late to quit."

I looked at Sowerby out of the corner of my eye. She could kick us out of the school for doing a skit we hadn't asked her permission to do. Especially this skit.

The little kids piped their way through a Russian song, then a Chinese one. A wave of applause broke out. A lovely black haired senior who was engaged to a boy in the Air Force, followed them. She clasped her hands in front of her and sang, "I'll Walk Alone."

"I really do feel sick," I muttered. Turning to Kat, "We're going to get in so much trouble from doing this."

"Shhh," Anne hissed.

"Quit having hysterics," Kat said.

"But you said yourself they won't like our message. I saw their faces out there. Nothing we say is going to change their minds. So what's the use?"

Kat folded her arms and looked down at me. "Rosemary, you're being just plain chicken." Her voice was cold. "Your grandfather would be ashamed of you."

I wrung my hands and moaned.

"Shhh," Anne said again.

The senior finished singing and walked off to loud applause. Sowerby gestured to me. I pretended I didn't see her. My name was next on the program.

Kat stalked out onto the stage. Her curly hair was hidden under one of her father's brown hats. David's tan trench coat was belted around her slender waist. Gripping a notebook, she said in a dull monotone, "This is a true story, but we've changed the names of the people who lived through this nightmare . . ."

A burst of laughter exploded out of the front row. Behind them, someone gasped. Something—the laughter or the gasp— made Kat freeze. She gripped the mike so tight her knuckles turned pale, but she didn't open her mouth.

Anne muttered to me, "She's paralyzed. Get out there and help her."

My feet felt like they were ankle deep in cement. Anne shoved me, but I still couldn't move. Then from high above me, a loud voice yelled, "Go!"

That voice broke the spell. I walked out and sat down on the chair Kat had placed in the center of the stage for me to sit on. I sat down. Kat was still staring goggle eyed into the footlights. I groaned. Kat didn't move. I groaned again louder. Finally Kat turned to look at me.

"So, Mrs. Goldwasser," she said. Someone giggled. "My newspaper wants to know what conditions are like for Jews in Germany."

"*Mein kinder*," I bent over like someone with a stomachache, moaning, "*mein kinder*."

Kat started scribbling in her notebook.

I began on the long speech I'd rehearsed for weeks. "My son Isaac is ten, a good boy, wearing his yellow Star of David on his coat. His broken arm is in a cast and he's walking home, he's not making trouble, just trying to get home." I was so deep in the part, my voice broke as I said this. "But then a Nazi officer calls out 'Heil Hitler,'" my voice got louder, "and mein lieber Isaac . . ."

Someone in the front row said, "My *ham* sandwich, I dropped my *ham* sandwich." Followed by giggles. And hissing. Another voice. "*Mein* liverwurst sandwich."

Laughter.

Miss Sowerby rose up from her seat in the back. Angrily she said, "I'm giving a bad conduct mark to every girl in the first row. All of you will leave the auditorium, now."

Still laughing, the club clattered noisily up the aisle. The auditorium was quiet now, but my mind had gone blank. People rustled their programs and coughed, but I had no idea what to say next.

From the wings Anne shouted, "When I say Heil Hitler, boy, you salute!"

Somehow I got going again. I finished my speech by crying, "Isaac, Isaac, talk to me, talk to me!"

When it was over, I stood up. Nobody clapped. I walked off the stage.

Anne walked out, dressed in fancy black clothes, but moving like a sleepwalker, as if she had cobwebs over her eyes.

Kat took her arm and guided her to the chair, "Mrs. Friedman can you tell us your story?" Anne turned her head and looked around blankly. "Mrs. Friedman," Kat said sharply, "can you hear me?"

"I hear the fountains of my house in Berlin," Anne said singsong, "I hear my golden harp, I hear my canaries singing in their cages . . ." Tears rolled down her chalk white cheeks, "why should I listen to you?"

When Kat asked Anne to show what the Nazis had done to her, she flashed to her feet. She was dressed in the typical outfit of a rich woman, with a fur stole and hat, earrings and bracelets all borrowed from Mrs. Goodman. One by one she took things off, telling the audience how the Nazis stole her jewelry, her furs, her boots and hat and even her black lace dress. Finally Anne stood shivering on the stage dressed in a gray silk slip. "They left me no children. Nothing," she said. Kat led her offstage. Again, nobody clapped.

"You were great!" I patted Anne's arm.

"You too," Anne replied, still shivering.

"I'd have never made it, if you hadn't yelled 'Go.'"

"I didn't yell 'Go.'" Anne's dark eyes widened. "All I did was feed you that Heil Hitler line."

"Then who . . . ?" I stopped. My heart started beating really fast as I realized what had happened. Just when I needed it most, my inner voice had finally spoken up.

Kat walked back to face the audience. "We've told you the truth about what's happening to Jews in Germany today. We wanted you to see what could happen here unless we win this war."

There was light clapping. Someone whistled. Probably David. We took one bow and got off the stage fast.

Kat drooped. "They didn't clap much."

Anne said, "People don't clap for bad news."

Kat said, "People don't clap if the bad news happens to Jews. They don't care what happens to Jews." She hunched her shoulders and lowered her head.

I gave her arm a squeeze. We three had stood up for what we believed, the same as Teddy did at the war rally. Trying to smile, I said, "Hey, we did our best. We told them what's going on . . ."

Slowly Kat nodded. Anne too. I got a peaceful feeling inside. We'd performed our skit and we'd survived. Hallelujah!

Soon Sowerby would punish us for putting on a skit without permission. Soon my poor mother would try to pretend she wasn't panicked about my social future. Soon the club girls would mock us. But right now, I was feeling really good.

Everything happened just like I thought. Sowerby bawled us out. But she didn't actually punish us and she definitely didn't suspend us or kick us out. The club girls went around talking about *ham sandwiches,* but a couple of their members started to come up to the science lab to eat lunch with Anne, Kat and me.

After the performance, Mum whispered, "You made me cry," and patted me gently on the back. When she tried to greet Lucy's mother, Mrs. Lavalle turned her head and walked by as if my mother were invisible. While I stood there, clenching my fists, our history teacher

112

came up and said, "Girls, you're going to look back on today and feel proud of yourselves."

I didn't tell her we already felt proud.

Friday, June 19, 1942
Diplomat Ship Arrives with 92 Refugees from Nazi Prisons
10,000 Women Rush to Join New Army Corps

Chapter Twenty-Five

Two things happened in June. One was Miss Worth's Graduation Dance. Kat looked an absolute knockout in a black and white crepe dress from Hattie Carnegie. Yves came through with a great blind date for her—Peter, a six foot tall blond guy from California. The two of them started gabbing about Venice Beach and Malibu and when Peter asked her to dance, Kat stood up without mentioning her leg.

They danced slowly and people watched them because they made a great looking couple. Yves punched me and made the "V for Victory" sign. I grinned back.

Mona's date kept looking at Kat. He stared so hard he forgot to move his big feet. With a furious look, Mona pushed him over to the punch bowl.

When the band struck up "Good Night Ladies," Yves pulled me close. We finished the evening dancing cheek to cheek.

The other important thing happened on the last day of school. Kat and I walked down the street to Einstein's house.

When he turned the corner and came toward us, I spoke up fast before I lost my nerve. "Professor Einstein, I used to live across the street from you." I pointed to my old house. "This is my friend Kat Goodman. She's from California and she's a scientist and she wants to meet you."

Einstein took his pipe out of his mouth and said, "Ah." Then he said, "California is a very beautiful state. Once I lived there."

Now it was Kat's turn to talk, but her face was shiny with sweat and her brown eyes were popping. She swallowed, but nothing came out. Finally she cleared her throat and managed to croak, "I want to go to Cal Tech."

Einstein nodded. "That is where I almost took a job, until they offered me a special opportunity here in Princeton." He looked at Kat and his hooded eyes were kind. "After the war, science will have need of such as you. Don't let anyone persuade you out of your dreams."

"I-I won't."

When he went inside his house, Kat jumped up and down, pounding my back. "Wow, I spoke to Einstein, I actually spoke to him! Thanks pal. If I ever get the chance to name an experiment or something, I'm naming it after you."

I laughed, thinking of my first day in the lab, "You mean Rosemary's Ruin?"

"No," Kat said seriously, "I'm calling it the Hoyt Solution."

The Hoyt Solution. I liked the sound of that. Once I'd counted on Einstein to solve my problems. Now I knew I could handle things on my own.

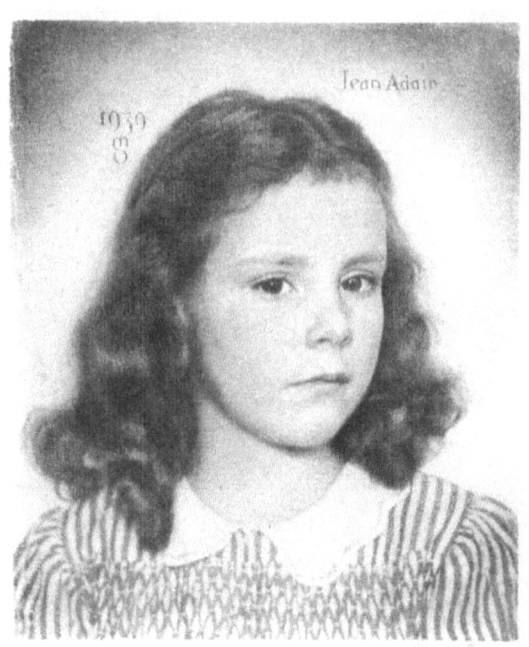

About the Author

Jean Adair Shriver loves children and books. She used to live in an old house on the East Coast. Now she lives in an old house on the West Coast surrounded by children and books and peacocks. She's proud that once she lived across the street from Albert Einstein (named Person of the Century in 1999), but she's still a dud at algebra. She has published one previous book, *Mayflower Man*.